With Sacred Honor

Also Available from J.B. Solomon Editions

Anywhere but Here
Stories by Tim Bugansky

In the Hardship and the Hoping: Poems of Northeast Ohio
Poems by Various Authors

Screaming Freedom
Poems by Allen Michael Hines

With Sacred Honor

a novel by

William T. Johnson

J.B. Solomon Editions
Alliance, Ohio

Branch Adult Fiction
Johnson, W
Johnson, William T
With sacred honor

© 2011 by William T. Johnson
All rights reserved.

This is a work of fiction. Any resemblance to actual people, places, or events is purely coincidental or is used fictitiously.

ISBN 978-0-578-09873-9
Library of Congress Control Number: 2011963118

J.B. Solomon Editions
Alliance, Ohio
jbsolomoneditions@yahoo.com

For Hobbs' Company, now and then

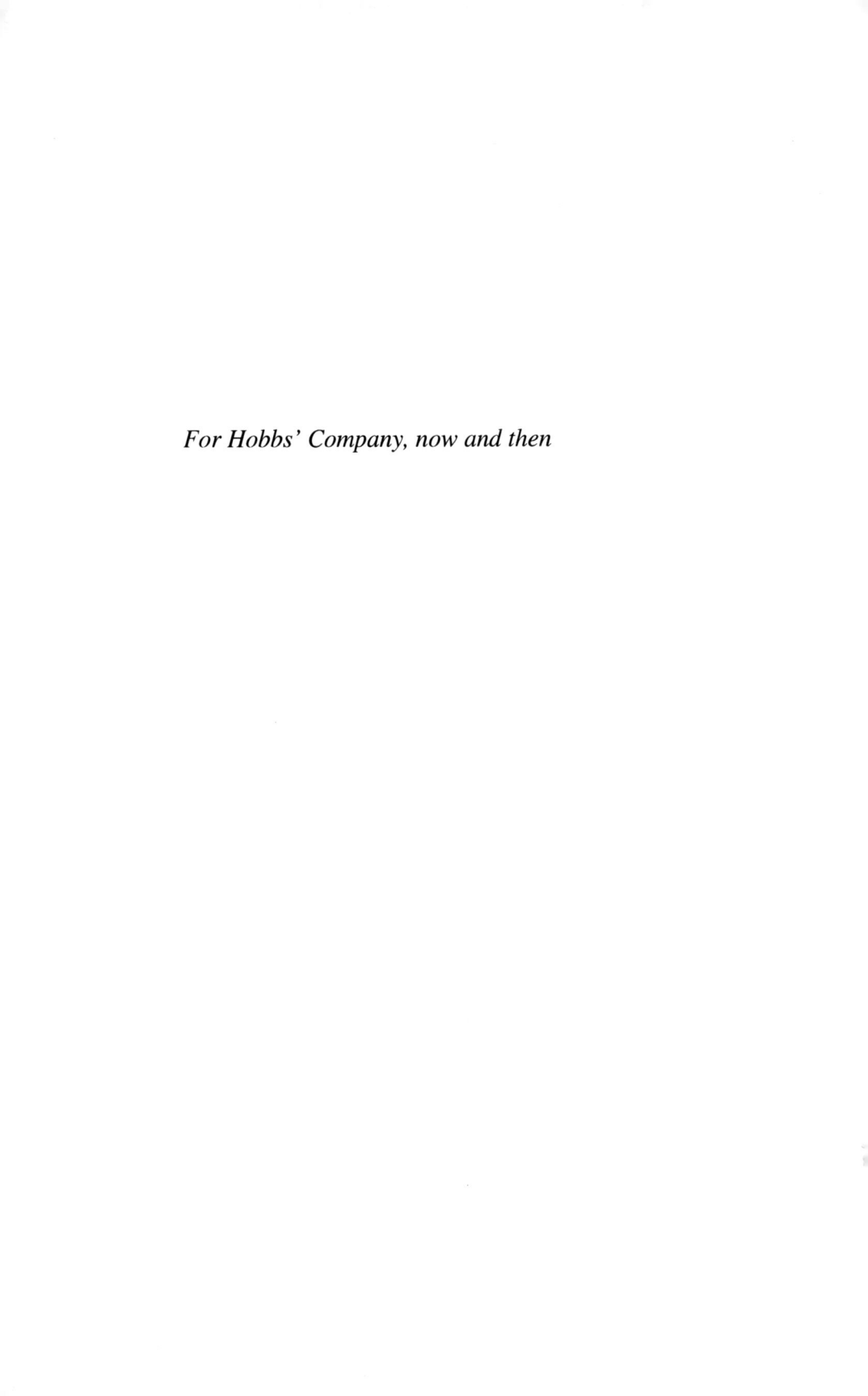

Editor's Note

Nestled along a curve in the road in rural Northeast Ohio is a welcoming, weather-worn cabin. Its hewn-wood walls have borne their burden for well more than a century, and its creaking floors whisper secrets from the past.

On autumn evenings – evenings such as the one on which your present author pens these words of introduction – the nostalgic, melancholy smell of woodsmoke drifts through the air and clings to the cabin in a gentle, arresting embrace that is at once immediate and timeless.

Our author, William T. Johnson, dwells in this cabin. As does Solomon, the protagonist of *With Sacred Honor*. The reader will no doubt already have noted the similarity of Solomon's name with that of the press which brings you his tale. When J.B. Solomon Editions began to take shape several years ago, Solomon and his story were at the heart of the endeavor. It was always our intention to bring Johnson's manuscript to the public, and over the past few years we have been steadily striving to do so.

Solomon's tale, however, is one that has been more than a few years in the making. In fact, Solomon and his world are the work of a lifetime. Far more than a two-dimensional character, Solomon is a protagonist whom Johnson has discovered as much as he has developed – and Solomon, in turn, has imbued Johnson's own life with untold significance and perspective. Solomon is both a distillation and a point of departure, and Johnson has used his discoveries to enrich the understanding of countless individuals and audiences with whom he has crossed paths. An intrepid traveler; an accomplished re-enactor who has contributed his talents to numerous nationally aired documentaries; and a skillful public speaker, naturalist, and storyteller, Johnson has labored to share his knowledge with others – and he remains always open to new ideas and points of view with which to inform his ever-broadening understanding of the past and how it has shaped, and continues to shape, our present world.

A driven and ever-curious scholar, Johnson has spent decades immersing himself in the lore and lifestyles of the newcomers who carved homes for themselves in colonial North America, as well as the Native American cultures who preceded them, co-existed with them, and came into conflict with them. Johnson has come to focus particularly upon the French and Indian War, a critical period that was the culmination of events, ideas, and ambitions that had shaped the political landscape of North America up to that point – and whose undercurrents and repercussions set the stage for the birth of the United States a few short years later.

The French and Indian War – acknowledged by many scholars as the first truly "world war" – convulsed the globe and saw the world's preeminent powers locked in a bitter struggle at whose heart lay the Ohio Country, Johnson's lifetime home. Johnson understands and passionately shares with others the significance of that global conflagration. Furthermore, he possesses a keen appreciation for the role Native American nations played as actors in their own right in that pivotal drama, rather than as the two-dimensional pawns many popular accounts have painted them.

Within the French and Indian War, Johnson's area of special interest is the Stockbridge Indians of Massachusetts, a tribe that remained fiercely loyal to the English cause during a period when wary Native Americans strategically shifted allegiances according to what they perceived best suited their positions in the North American political balance – and would best ensure their futures as free and independent peoples.

Out of that interest has sprung Solomon. Johnson has brought him alive in countless presentations and historical reenactments. Solomon has come to be an integral part of everything Johnson endeavors to do, both informing and being informed by our author's own life. Solomon is the product of and driving force behind Johnson's rambles along cobblestoned colonial streets and his treks up New England mountain peaks. Johnson has spent many a midnight poring over archival manuscripts and many a midwinter's day creeping through the snow-draped woods, his feet clad in moccasins and his senses seeking new knowledge about what life may have been like centuries ago.

Solomon lives, indeed. His home is about the hearth of Johnson's sturdy cabin and in the heart of our ever-curious author. It is in the pages of the tale which shall shortly unfold before you. And hopefully, Solomon and his companions will also soon dwell in the imagination of you, our esteemed reader.

I.

The moon shines warmly tonight in this place that I have come to accept as my home. Wisps of smoke drift from the chimneys of the other cabins, but most of the villagers have let their hearths cool and have retired to their beds for slumber. But I cannot sleep. Another night spent surrounded by memories and the ghosts of departed brothers. I think that tonight would be a good one to be in the woods again, but my body, riddled with aches and old wounds, will not allow me to sleep on the naked ground as once I often did.

My hand extends to the rough planks of my unpainted door. I slide the bolt with my left and reach with my right. When my palm makes contact, I can feel the furry oak grain as I increase my pressure, making the iron hinges surrender to my will. Warm, smoky air eases past me when the door is cast aside; the sounds of autumn rush in through the entrance that I nearly fill. It is not that my frame is large – quite the opposite as a result of these long years – but that the doorway, in proportion to the cabin, is small. A balance is reached between inside and out, making the sense of escaping heat disappear and unbending the flames of the fire in the hearth. Now that the door is not braced by the frame, a light breeze catches it and softly rocks it back and forth. The hinges emit a metallic creaking. I make note to acquire grease from the blacksmith.

Few people stir in this late hour. A figure, across the clearing which stands between the double row of closely huddled cabins, silently returns with pails of water from the spring. By the task and what I can see of the wraith-like shadow I suppose that it is Ruth from down the way. She does not see me. And then I am suddenly alone again. Alone – a relative term, as all of the cabins around me are occupied, but a condition that is determined more by emotion than actual proximity to other beings. At different times I have felt accompanied when the nearest persons were far below me and out of view; and at other times alone while another slept in my arms.

A ring of light circles the moon in the sky and I close my eyes to murmur a small prayer of Thanksgiving. I ask the Lord to grant me strength of memory. Tomorrow I will gather with the others in the small framed church and we will sing our praise to God. Many will give hollow benedictions to Him for their fortunes; but my words to God are sacred, wholehearted if weary thanks for surviving the many occurrences in which I have seen both His grace and His wrath.

Opening my eyes, I slowly stroke the long gray locks that splay over my shoulders and I wonder when they turned from their shining ebony to this old man's adornment. I am suddenly shaken from my reminiscence as a loud whoop rings down the corridor between the two lines of cabins. I reach for and feel the small knife I keep tucked in the sash at my waist. It is the only weapon that I have retained over the years, vowing that if Death comes to visit as oft times before, I will greet Him with this alone. I see that it is a few young men who have returned from their raid with some horses from across the river. I don't care to hear the news. Despite my advanced age, I have not attained the status of a venerated elder. After our last removal, I stopped telling my stories; few know the paths that I have traversed. To most, I know, I am the eccentric – deranged, perhaps – old man who drinks too much and sometimes wakes them up with his midnight screams. I live alone, and I have been alone in all the time that these people have known me. At times, they have seen the odd figure arrive at my door and enter it without knocking; strange persons, some speaking few words of English, some missing body parts, and some with the same long and distant stare that plagues me.

To get by, I occasionally sell one of the old muskets with inscrutable foreign stamp-marks or one of the many other trinkets that serve as painful reminders of the deeds of my youth. Sometimes I pay for needed supplies with ancient Spanish Pieces-of-Eight or various other exotic currencies. The days have passed when young men provided for the needy, old, or infirm.

The hour is late now, late for all but especially for me. Swiftly I approach my final silence, the silence when, even if they should be willing, no one will be able to hear of these things that I have seen and done. It is Time's promise that each man will be forgotten. In defiance of this law, men struggle to be remembered. Some commit this act in purely selfish fashion, but in my way I have always attempted to diverge from that path. Many times, unfortunately, I have failed in my attempts at humility; I am, after all, a mere man of flesh and sin. But in this final chance to explain, I will show that these advanced years have only been attained through the deeds of many great men and women. If not for their selflessness, their bravery, and their sacrifice, these words would not have found you. So now, friends, fill your glasses and draw near your fires – draw near my fire. By morning, the muskets might once again shout their angry cries in the fields and houses of this small village – or, Lord forbid, your own. Yes, fill your glasses; *we may or might never all meet here again*. And I have much to tell.

II.

When I was old enough to listen and remember, my grandmother would tell me the story of my birth. It was very cold, she would recall, and more snow had fallen than in many years before.

"Your mother was strong, you know, Solomon. Strong like Abigail."

I looked up from the small fire burning in Grandmother's wigwam to Abigail who, as always, did not react to Grandmother's words. She kept snapping the long beans, throwing the ends into the fire and the bodies into a large, wooden bowl balanced on her legs.

"I think she knew that she would not live to see another sunrise when she began her pains with you. The look was in her eyes. She continued, fearless in her efforts to bring you into the world and when you came – oh, little one, when you came you could not have knocked the smile from her face!"

I was proud for a moment. Proud in the way that youth allows us to forget the rest of a story. I beamed a smile at Grandmother and she returned it with her own, sad smile. I noticed that Abigail's hands had stopped working and I looked over at her again. Her jaw was set tight to hold back the tears and I was caught by that image. And I remembered the consequence of my bearing.

"Now, you two lose those faces!" Grandmother ordered. "Your mother would have nothing to do with her passing making you all sad. No tears. No tears, little ones.

"She would have changed nothing. It is not ours to change. These are the ways of the Creator," Grandmother explained in her soothing voice.

"I'm not crying, Momasis," I told her.

"I know, Solomon. You are a brave Mohican warrior! Now then, my water gourds appear to be empty. I wonder if there is anyone strong enough to fill them and carry them back from the spring?"

"I can!" I exclaimed as I jumped to my feet, nearly upsetting Abigail's bowl. This is the way that Grandmother was able to get many things done. There was never an order, nor even a request. Simply a question floated on the air, a question that was always rapidly responded to by any number of her grandchildren laying about her wigwam.

I gathered together the various gourds as Grandmother pulled them from this and that place. In the end, she produced a half dozen of them, neat little things colored yellow by age. Each had a finely woven rope handle strung through the top and a small hole bored in the side. Others of these that had grown old or become cracked hung in the trees about Grandmother's lodge. Wrens found these to be excellent homes, filling them with grass and, later, eggs no larger than a child's eye. When things no longer fulfilled their original purpose, Grandmother often found other uses for them; nothing was wasted or cast aside as useless.

With my tiny hands slipped through the various handles I stepped outside into the clear air. Trails of smoke followed me from the interior of the wigwam and I watched them quickly disperse in the soft breeze of early fall. I have heard that people love most the season into which they are born, but I found this to be untrue for myself. Even in these early years, I found wonder in two seasons: spring and, as it was on that day, fall. To this day, the sight of dry corn stalks standing in fields and the multitude of colors worn by the trees makes my heart stir in a peculiar way akin to falling in love.

The gourds were light in my hands as the leaves crunched under my bare feet and cold mud pushed between my toes. Other people, mostly women and children, were making their way to the spring, as well, and the many trails dwindled to one as we neared it. Also along the way was the large field where the older boys would play lacrosse. As I passed, I saw the boys were gathered together in a group, devising their plan of attack. Briefly their attention was turned when the smallest in their group spied me walk by. James was often picked on by the others because of his size, and he missed no chance to refocus this unwanted attention to those smaller and weaker than him.

"Look at Solomon! He is practicing to be a girl carrying water!" he cried in an insulting voice. "Hey, Solomon – will you help my sister bring us water as well?"

I walked faster, trying to outdistance him and his attention. The other boys laughed, which only served to feed James' taunts. Now he was beside me, trotting backward and yelling his taunts so that his friends could hear. "Your sister Abigail brought water to my wigwam last night. She tried to get me to go down by the river with her but I told her that I was busy."

When I grew older I learned to ignore people like James, but when young I was unable to let the insult pass. I froze in my tracks. My hands were filled with the rope handles of the gourds that dangled at my side, and my mind raced for something to retort. I had never been quick to respond in such situations, but when I did my words were most often beyond brutal.

"Speaking of my sister, she told me that your mother was an Abenaki slave that the Iroquois gave to your father. Is that true?" I asked, bracing my tone with innocence.

I already knew the question to be true. I also knew that it was unnecessary to draw upon such ugliness for my gain, but it was I who was cornered. James drew back his ball stick to strike me, but the leader of his team ran up and pulled him back to the game.

"Let's go, James. It's time to play again." He spoke this with the elegance of redirection that so many peacemakers employ.

I gathered my gourds and continued on to the spring, sensing James' hot gaze on my back. As I carried on, I felt badly about being so mean toward James, but I could not remain silent at his remarks. So go the paths of many conflicts in our lives. We desire them not, but seem powerless to avoid them.

When I returned to Grandmother's wigwam the beans had all been cleaned and sorted. Our earlier conversation had not left Abigail unscathed, and I saw the two sitting and embracing as I approached. Grandmother was singing a sweet, soft song to Abigail and the two rocked gently back and forth near the low-burning fire.

"Were there many people at the spring?" Grandmother asked as I hung the gourds around her lodge.

"A few," I answered as I looked down at my sister as she brushed tears from her face with her sleeve. "Grandpa Heron was telling his stories to the children beside the spring. ... And James tried to fight me again."

Abigail jumped to her feet at the mention of James and asked if he was talking about her.

"Abigail. Solomon. Don't you two be getting drawn into that awful child's evil medicine," Grandmother instructed. "His father has not taken a bow to that boy's backside enough times, and I'll not have you two encouraging his hatefulness. Both of you will find enough worthy things to quarrel about as you grow older. Let him be angry, and do not let him poison your hearts. Do you understand?"

Abigail and I both nodded our heads but our youthful anger still burned hot, as could be seen in our twisted faces.

And then, just as quickly as our emotions had turned sour, Abigail and I were distracted by a haggard looking family that had just entered the village. Grandmother saw them, too, and after a moment of assessing them she remembered her manners and instructed us to go help them.

As I approached, I could see that the man who was leading the group appeared ill. His face was ash-colored – like what remains after an all-night fire. A woman and a little girl followed after him. The girl was tightly holding the woman's hand. My eyes returned to the man. He had no musket but he was carrying a small canvas bag over his shoulder that seemed alarmingly empty. His eyes were downcast, and every few moments he stopped to wipe the sweat from his forehead. He looked sick, yet dangerous in some small way, so I passed him up and went to the woman. She was carrying a small copper kettle containing rough, wooden spoons and a half-eaten loaf of bread. Across her shoulders she bore several blankets tied up with a rope; the load seemed to weigh her down more than it should as she, too, was staring at the ground.

"Good day," I greeted her, meeting her gaze when she heard me approach. She smiled thinly at my greeting.

"Can I help you with that?" I asked as I reached up and touched the rope around her shoulders.

"What a nice young man," she replied. "Yes, you may help me."

The young girl at her side buried her face in the woman's petticoats and I could hear her sobbing through the coarse cloth. I slumped the blankets over my shoulders and turned to see Grandmother and Abigail converging near the man. I fell in step behind the woman and girl and listened to Grandmother speaking to the man as we came alongside him.

"Newly arrived are you?" Grandmother inquired sweetly.

The man barely nodded his head. He began to reply, but his words were caught in his throat as he barked a loud cough. When he caught his breath, he explained that they had been walking for days and had enjoyed little shelter – and even less food.

"Well then, no one walks by this lodge hungry," Grandmother said in her happiest voice as she waved them toward her home. Though my eyes might have betrayed me, the look of danger on the man's face seemed to evaporate to a simple countenance of absolute exhaustion and total loss of pride.

My Grandmother did all that she could to make the small family comfortable as she seated them near her fire. From the rafters of her lodge, she procured several baskets full of bread and dried vegetables. Within moments of their being seated, she had the fire crackling merrily and placed large wooden bowls in each of their laps. Each bowl was filled with the aromatic stew that she had been preparing before their arrival. Between ravenous mouthfuls, the man introduced himself as Edward and told us the names of his wife and daughter.

"That is Elizabeth," he said, indicating his wife with a wave of his hand.

"And this little angel is Catherine," he explained with a smile and a pat on the head of the little girl seated beside him.

It was the first time that the girl looked up from her bowl at me. My heart skipped a beat as I saw her beautiful eyes. They were green like the emeralds that I had once viewed in the dry, cracked hands of a trader who had come to our village. Her eyebrows turned down when she noticed me staring at her and she stuck out her tongue at me to show her displeasure. Had this been any other girl, I would have probably stuck my tongue out in kind, but this moment caught me off guard and I was hurt by her rebuff.

"Enough of that, Catherine," her father ordered. She tucked her head down at his sharp words and returned to her eating. I looked away and saw Grandmother smirking at my surprised face.

"Looks like this wood pile is getting small," Grandmother commented. I took the suggestion and pulled myself up to my feet, trying to look dignified in the way a child does when he has been injured.

"I'll get some more, Momasis," I told her, putting on my most helpful voice.

"Ask Reverend Sargent if that little cabin by the church is still empty, too," Grandmother added. I hurried out of Grandmother's lodge so that no one else, especially Abigail, would see my injured look.

A new feeling was in my heart as I walked between the rows of lodges and cabins looking for the reverend. Now that ten summers had passed since I was born, I had begun to notice girls in a different way. But this girl – and the way I felt instantly drawn to her – was completely unlike anything I had ever experienced. It was difficult to focus on where I should gather wood or find Reverend Sargent or even where to place my feet. My thoughts were wholly consumed by the image that I had in my mind of those two beautiful eyes. I passed others – including my friend Jacob, who hailed me heartily – but barely noticed them. The only thing that I was aware of was a small vibration that seemed to be boiling to the surface of my skin from deep inside my body. I shook my head, cleared my thoughts, and set off purposefully to do what I had been asked – and anything else I could think of to help this girl and her parents.

III.

Six winters had come and gone since the arrival of Catherine and her parents. Six hard snows that packed the ground and left lodges and cabins lean of meat as the deer became scarcer in the round hills and deep forests that surrounded Stockbridge, our mission village in the west of the colony of Massachusetts. Adding to the hardships of food shortages was the danger of raids by war parties from the north. These war parties were made up of Abenakis and Frenchmen sent from Quebec to make trouble with English villagers and their Indian brothers. Militias were formed of the townsmen in each village; these did their best to repel these marauders. But when the militias employed the tactics of European warfare, their efforts were often in vain against Indian-style fighting. The colonists had learned to stand in lines, facing other men formed in similar lines, and fire in orderly volleys.

    The Abenaki and their French allies, however, chose to fight in the way that we Indians have always fought: to find a good rock or tree to hide behind and direct each arrow or musket ball at a particular man. There were no orderly lines or volleys. Each man acted as he best saw fit, independent of his fellows but against a common enemy. This style of warfare was closely related to the way that men hunt animals. Consequently, as had been seen fit during periods of past conflict, our English brothers compelled us Mohicans to meet the enemy in our Indian fashion of battle. The young warriors from our village made raids against the Abenaki and French villages in the same way that the Abenaki had been attacking us and our friends. Often, warriors from Stockbridge would travel to Pittsfield, a large town to the north, to obtain from the English muskets, lead, and other provisions to outfit their war parties. Through the influence of Sir William Johnson, the Iroquois to the west of our village joined the Stockbridge Indians in these raids against our enemies. Soon, the entire existence of the Mohawks, members of the Iroquois Confederacy who lived nearest to us, became dependent on the English to provide for them, not only for warfare but also for everyday living.

Fortunately, because Stockbridge was a village made up of both whites and Indians living together, our white brothers encouraged us to continue caring for our own needs and not become solely beholden to the British army for our sustenance. It came to pass in those years that there was not always fighting to be found, and the army was less willing to part with provisions to help out the many Iroquois villagers. Some of the Iroquois people became very poor, but because we had held onto some of our old trades, we were better off than our western friends. One day, a few of the Mohawks came to ask how we managed to get by in these lean times. The men of this delegation were dispersed amongst us so that we could show them how we made baskets and brooms and other things that we were able to sell or trade. I was paired with Crow Wing, a young man about my age, so that I could explain how brooms were made, a trade that I had taken on in the past two years. His hair was plucked back to a neat scalp-lock at the top of his head, and his arms, legs, and chest were covered in the tattoos of a warrior. He was dressed in the manner of a warrior rather than a tradesman. Bright red wool leggings covered his legs, and below each knee was tied a thick belt of wampum. The white, frilled shirt he wore was covered with red paint at the shoulders – remnants of war expeditions past – and silver brooches adorned the front. He quickly grew bored at my instruction of how to secure the handle between one's legs and hold the straws just so. He asked if I ever had the occasion to hunt. He said this in challenging manner as he cast his half-finished broom to the ground and grabbed his musket, which had been leaning against a tree just outside my cabin door.

"You do not care to see what I'm showing you?" I asked impatiently.

"Women make brooms and baskets," he replied.

I eyed him, annoyed that he would come here for help but not listen. I tried to continue my lesson but he would only stand with his arms folded across his chest, cradling the barrel of his firelock and staring off at the distance hills. I decided it was pointless to continue in my instruction until I had gained his respect as a man.

"All right, Crow Wing. We'll go hunt," I conceded. I threw my unfinished broom down next to his and went into my cabin to get my quiver of arrows and my bow. When I returned outside, he was smiling and ramming a ball down the barrel of his gun. I could not help but smile, too.

"To tell you the truth," I started, "I get tired of sitting around here making these damn things. I'd rather be in woods."

He laughed and slapped me on the back as his other hand slid his ramrod back into the thimbles below the barrel of his gun.

"Solomon, where are you off to?" inquired Abigail as she returned with a basketful of corn. "I thought you were supposed to be showing our friend how to make brooms."

"We are going hunting!" I replied, a huge smile splitting my face. Abigail shook her head and placed the basket down at her feet.

"Now, you know ..." she started.

"Enough, sister. We're going hunting. Have something good cooking when we return," I ordered in a tone that I knew I should not take with her.

"Boy, you might live in this cabin, but you are not my man to be telling me what to do," she said angrily at the back of my head as Crow Wing and I trotted off.

"She is even more beautiful when she's angry," mused Crow Wing as we continued toward the edge of the village.

He had seen Abigail when he first came to our cabin for his lesson and had talked about her more than the broom-making throughout our lesson. I shot him an overly dramatic frown and elbowed him in the ribs before I took off at a full sprint toward the woods. I intended to outpace him into the forest, but I was brought to a standstill as I rounded the church. Standing in the middle of the path was Catherine. She was speaking to her father, who had never fully regained his health in all the preceding years in Stockbridge. After they had settled in, I had faithfully provided meat and whatever else I could manage to assist them. Catherine and I had become fast friends, and I took every possible opportunity to speak with her or spend time in her company.

Crow Wing rounded the corner and nearly collided with me.

"Good day, Solomon," Catherine greeted me. "Where are you two boys headed?"

"Hunting," I answered, always short of words when in her presence.

Catherine looked between Crow Wing and me, and then turned back to her father, seemingly uninterested.

"Aren't you supposed to be teaching our Mohawk friend how to make brooms?" Edward inquired. Despite his wrecked health, he had risen as a sort of headman in our church and village. His accusatory gaze and tone had taken me aback, and I searched my thoughts for an acceptable answer.

"Oh sir, we're done. I thought I'd show Crow Wing our beautiful forests before he has to return to his village," I lied.

Catherine looked at us with a skeptical gaze and a small smirk parting her beautiful lips.

"Well then, you boys be cautious," Edward warned. "These hills seem to be inundated with Abenaki and their papist conspirators these days."

"Thank you, sir," I replied in my most respectful voice.

Though it was I who provided for him, I had never lost my respect for his position as the father of my most beloved. I doubted that he knew my strong feelings for Catherine, or how she had thanked me on numerous occasions by taking my hand and kissing me with her soft lips. My fondest memory was of the time when she had asked that I join her down by the small river that ran along the edge of our village. The night had been severely black, illuminated but slightly by a sliver of moon. Catherine had come to my door and tapped softly on it until I opened it.

"Hello, Solomon," she had said. "Will you walk with me?"

I wrapped an old gray blanket around my waist and took her hand as she led me through the tall grass growing in a fallow field at the edge of the village. I gazed at her small back and tightly braided hair as the trail guided us through the field and onto the banks of the river. Her other arm was looped through the handle of a basket that had the neck of a violin protruding through the top. When she had decided on a place for us to stop, she asked me to lay my old blanket on the ground and bid me to sit down next to her. I needed no convincing and complied without a word. The warmth of her body next to mine sent a thrill deep into my soul. We sat in this way, without uttering a word, for some time. Her head rested lightly on my shoulder and my arm encircled her back.

"Solomon," she began.

My name sounded like a song from heaven floating on her sweet voice.

"Solomon ... You have been kind to me and my family since we arrived so many years ago."

She let this observation settle between us before she continued.

"Because of your care, we have never wanted for food or shelter or good company as long as we have been here. You have complimented me with your attention, and I see what hides behind your eyes when you look at me."

The depth of her insight made my hands shake with anticipation as I wondered what else she would say.

"I want to thank you for all that you have done," she continued.

With that said, she rose to her feet and drew the violin from the basket. She held the small, elegant instrument near her hip as she drew the tiny bow across its strings. A single note rose from the instrument as I closed my eyes to absorb whatever wondrous melody she would create. From that first note continued a soft but stirring reel that captivated my mind and thrilled my heart. The song she played brought tears to my eyes as I moved my head to its rhythm. When she had finished, she replaced the violin in the basket and returned to sit facing me on the blanket. I enfolded her in my arms and kissed her. Her hands gently brushed over my cheeks and neck for what seemed a thousand years yet a time far too short for young lovers. Finally, she withdrew a bit and placed her face before mine.

"I love you, Solomon," she said in the most earnest voice I have ever heard.

"And I love you," I replied with matched sincerity.

We kissed again. I have never felt a greater need or want or desire as I did at that moment. If ever a man sought the definition of passion it would have been found right there on the riverbank. Each kiss grew more intense as our fingers explored each other's bodies, venturing into places unknown yet imagined for so many years.

Though we were young, we no less knew the great beauty of love as we were swept away like the waters of the river flowing by at our feet.

As I recall that time for you – now separated from it by heartache, warfare and death – it burns not one flame less than at the moment of its occurrence.

"*That* is *beauty*," I told Crow Wing not many moons afterward as I grabbed his arm and lightly stepped around father and daughter.

"Good luck in your hunt!" exclaimed Catherine as Crow Wing and I ran towards the woods.

The massive trees and huge, moss-covered boulders did little to impede Crow Wing and I as we rushed up a deer trail, nearing the top of the highest hill that crowned over Stockbridge. Early autumn winds wisped through the multicolored palette of leaves around us as we slowed our pace and fell into the measured step of hunters. Soon, we startled fewer birds and disturbed only the closest squirrels as our eyes sought out the movement of deer. It thrilled me to be away from the bustle of the village and to quiet my mind in this place that held greater reverence for me than any church I had ever attended. Here was God's splendor, His workshop where He tinted the summer's leaves angry red and golden yellow as He prepared His creation for winter's long sleep.

I turned in my tracks to look down the mountain at my village. I saw the people moving about in fields and between cabins and wigwams, most of them oblivious to the hunters who had just departed. All unknowing but Abigail, Edward, and my love. My heart raced from the run up to this place but pounded even more furiously as I thought of Catherine. My eyes searched the pathways and dirt roads until I could make out her small cabin near the church. She and her father were nowhere to be seen, but just the sight of her home made me weak with desire. My nose flared as my breathing settled and I drew in all the smells of my surroundings: crushed leaves underfoot, the pungent odor of pine, and my own salty sweat.

Crow Wing brought me back to our task as he made a low clicking sound, like that of a squirrel hulling a nut. Carefully I turned, my left hand grasping my bow and my right reaching back to take an arrow from its quiver. Crow Wing pointed his chin toward another hilltop not far from the one we occupied. I focused my eyes and saw three small does slowly walking and grazing in the small clearing below us. Without a word, he and I began our stalk. He moved off to my left and I walked a line that would take me in a wide arch and place me downwind of the does. Our movements were excruciatingly slow as we try not to startle our quarry. When I was within range to take a shot, I gently leaned against a tree to steady my arm and slightly adjusted my eyes so that I could see Crow Wing, now just a small figure in the distant trees. I waited until I saw him brace against a tree in same stance that I had taken. When I was satisfied that he was still, I drew the arrow back, bringing the fletching feathers to lightly brush against the right corner of my mouth. I aimed at the doe nearest to me, focusing on the area just behind her front leg so that my arrow would pierce her heart and lung, bringing a fast death. I closed my eyes to concentrate my thoughts and when I reopened them I was still aiming at the same place on the doe. Grandfather Heron had taught me this way of calming my mind, assuring me that it was necessary for making a good kill.

Before I released the arrow, I whispered a quick prayer: "Creator, thank you for this sacrifice." My prayer spoken, I opened my fingers that held the arrow and sent it on its way. The distance was great enough that I could actually see it make the small rise and then plunge into the deer's side, burying half its length into her. The other deer ran a moment after she was hit, instantly sensing danger. As Crow Wing and I had planned, they darted towards him. The crash of his musket being fired caused the remaining, uninjured deer to skid sideways and then fly away deep into the forest. The deer Crow Wing had shot crumbled to the ground instantly as the heavy ball crashed into it. But the deer that I shot had kept to its feet and began to race after its uninjured companion. A thick stream of blood pumped from her side as she rushed away and soon she was stumbling from the wound I had inflicted. I didn't move from my tree, but rather kept a close eye on her as she finally lay down to accept her death. This was something else that Grandfather Heron had taught me: that a chased creature will keep to its feet as long as it feels that it is pursued.

A few days later, Catherine and I once again found ourselves at the river's edge. I cradled her in my arms and stroked her ebony hair.

"Solomon, what do you think will happen here in the next few years?" she asked, gazing into my eyes. "I heard some of the men talking about how French traders are buying scalps from the Hurons and Abenakis. Do you think that trouble will ever come here? What will the warriors do if that happens?"

Her questions probed deeper into the unknown than my young mind could fathom. I spoke the only words that came to me, words from Grandfather Heron, one of our elders: "Maya-we-helan."

She drew her head away and looked at me quizzically.

"Everything is as it should be," I translated. I then showed her the brass bracelet that Grandfather Heron had given me when he first told me the story. The simple pattern that wrapped around the entire band was of a continuous wave.

"All life is a circle that contains its ups and downs; that is what Grandfather Heron says," I explained.

Catherine let this slide across her thoughts as she replaced her head to my chest and her finger traced the wave in my bracelet. I pointed as the little muskrat came back out of its hole beside the river and scanned the sky for owls. The muskrat then sat and chewed on a small branch; it knew Grandfather Heron's words and understood them better than I ever would.

That evening left Catherine and I sitting on the bank for hours upon end. The moon slowly sank in the blackness of the western horizon and the stars shown more brilliantly than at the moment of their creation.

But as I have said, that old demon of sorrow and disappointment eternally lurked and waited to ambush me. This experience was no different. One day when I had decided to go and visit with my friend, I was met with a note posted on her family's cabin door. Great disbelief was the first sensation that filled my mind as I read over and over these lines.

Dear Solomon,

My father's health has grown worse. We fear for his sake and despite all prayers and medicine he has not grown well. We have gone to Boston to seek help and are prepared to return to England if his health completely fails. I had hoped to see you before we left, but no time could be spared. I hope that you remain well and that I will see you again. Take care Solomon; you will do fine in life. It is my most fervent desire that our paths shall cross again.

Your Most Obdnt Srvt,
Catherine

When Catherine's words had set in and I became fully aware of their meaning, I vowed to myself that I would someday find her, though I had no idea how.

IV.

Abigail had not found a husband, so for the next few years I was obliged to provide for my dear sister. I also remained busy helping new arrivals to Stockbridge in the construction of their homes. But any chance that I got, I would disappear into the forest. Here I would acquire game, calm my mind, and continue to develop my familiarity with life in the woods. As I grew older, these stays in the wilderness grew longer and longer. I began to feel more at home there than in my own cabin. In those days, most men hunted with firelock muskets, but I was still young and hunted with a bow. The men that had firelocks had acquired them through trade or issue from the British Army. Many nights I would sit and listen to them speak of their experiences in battle, what they had seen and what they had done. Their stories were filled with accounts of their guns belching shot at their unfortunate enemies, with tales of capturing prisoners and outwitting other men. When I was on the hunt, these images would fill my mind and I would imagine that I was stalking a company of French Marines or a Huron war party. But no amount of imagining or daydreaming could prepare me for the bitter realities of life and what would befall me and those I loved.

    I clearly remember that spectacular fall day; it was the most incredible that I had ever seen. A dry summer had brought a quick and dramatic change to the leaves. Their color combining with the day's sun made the woods seem all the more dazzling. Each tree's leaves seemed so different from the next that the outline of them could be distinguished one from the other. As I crawled under a fallen tree I scooped a handful of dried leaves. I pressed them to my face to absorb the true scent of the coming season.

I had just killed a large doe and dressed it out to carry back to the village to share her sacrifice with all, as is the way of the People. I moved through the variety of colors as if floating through a lake of vermilion and gold. As I neared the village, it struck me that the smell of smoke was much stronger than most days. Usually I would smell the fires of the village's chimneys as I approached, but not at this distance. I had not heard talk before I left of clearing land, but I knew that this could be a possibility. It was common to burn trees to make way for new fields. Nonetheless, for a moment I became nervous for Abigail. I shook off the feeling; but I quickened my step, knowing I was only a few ridges away from Stockbridge. I still had the deer on my shoulders and I thought about how she was still warm, its life not completely drained away. Her blood ran down the back of my linen shirt and along my arms, making my hands stick to my bow.

But all thoughts of the beautiful day, the deer, and the leaves left my mind as I crested the last hill and looked into the Housatonic Valley. There below me I beheld a scene that chilled my blood. The cabins were burning and children were screaming. I swept my gaze across the village – so near yet in that terrible moment so distant – and spied a woman whom I knew well, huddled over a small, bloody bundle on the ground.

I shirked the load from my shoulder and began running down the hillside. I had run hard in my life, but never like this. I felt no pain from my body as I pushed it well beyond its normal capabilities. My feet seemed to not touch the ground, and with each step the village grew larger before me. Thoughts of the village, the people, and most importantly my sister drove me forward like a star shooting across the night sky.

I crashed through the cornfield at the edge of the village. The knife-like leaves of the cornstalks did nothing to slow me. I reached back to my quiver and ripped an arrow forward, knocking it into the string on my bow. A voice in my head told me to slow down, but my heart would not allow any pausing or hesitation; thus, I pressed forward in a headlong rush. Pushing through the last few stalks, I knew that I would fight today; I knew that it would be soon. My right arm drew back the bow string and I asked the Creator to guide me in battle. Crashing from the field, I slammed into a painted warrior, sending my arrow wild. Every sense was heightened; I can still recall the smell of the bear grease paint that was slathered over his body. I heard his musket clatter to the ground, and my bow flew from hands. After a brief flight through the air our bodies detached and fell to the hard-packed earth. I looked up at him as I groped for my knife. I saw him doing the same. My other hand swept across one of my arrows that had splayed out of my quiver in the collision. I grasped it and gained my feet in the same motion. I was to him before he could scramble to his musket, which had fallen to the ground a few feet away. With all the strength I could employ, I plunged the arrow into his side. He screamed but kept true to his pursuit of his firelock, scrambling like a bear on all fours. I stumbled backward in disbelief that the arrow had not fazed him. I fell back and crushed my head into the ground; all went nearly dark for a moment, and then I leaned forward to see the warrior raising his musket to my face. I instinctually turned my head, awaiting the blast. I heard the crashing report from a musket and knew that I must be dead; no man looks down the barrel of a loaded gun and lives to speak of it if the gun speaks first.

It then occurred to me that I was still very much alive. I turned my gaze to see the painted man lying in crumpled ball a few yards away. Miraculously, I was unharmed. Time slowed in the next few minutes. I looked beyond the dead man and saw my unknown savior, a man I had never seen before. The vision of this blond, blue-eyed man pierced through me, even at a distance of thirty yards. His musket was shouldered and smoke was billowing from its steely maw. He covered the ground in no time and with his knife scalped the dead warrior. I had never seen a man scalped but had heard of it a hundred times over. Still, I sat on the ground in total disbelief of all that was occurring. In some combination of English and Irish, he screamed at me, ordering me to get to my feet. It was an order I had no problem following. In a slightly humoring voice he told me salvation comes but once. It was a message I had heard many times in the church – the same church that I could now see, at the edge of my vision, completely engulfed in flames. As the man gave me my message of salvation, he threw me the dead man's trade gun, covered in its former owner's blood. I thought of my bow and realized much more than weapons had changed for me in only an instant. The blond man edged close to me and snapped open the hammer and filled the pan of the trade gun, re-priming it. Then he slapped it shut.

"Follow me," he said.

I began to, but then grabbed his arm and said that I needed to find my sister. At this he nodded and replied, "Lead the way, boy."

We rounded a few cabins and came to my home. There I saw two painted figures wrestling with someone on the ground. They were trying to slip a rope around the person's wrists but were having great difficulty in their endeavor. I saw a foot fly up and slam into one of the warrior's breechcloth. He went limp and fell to ground; at this I could see the person they were trying to capture was Abigail. The second man continued to try to get the rope around her hands. Red had filled my vision and I knew what I was to do. Raising the musket to my shoulder I placed the silver lug at the end of the barrel so that it aimed at the back of the man's skull.

Then I took my first shot in anger. Bone, brain, and blood spattered on my sister's white shirt. I ran to her, helped her to her feet, and clutched her in a protective embrace. A second later, my new friend was at my heels, shouting at me to reload. I bent and took the powder horn and pouch from the man I had just killed. Even in that moment of absolute madness, I could not help but notice how the air was filled with the smells of the slaughter – the salty, rank stench of blood and the fetid stink of burst bowel. As I slunk from the scene, my new companion kicked the body over and pulled a sack of lead balls from a sash at the dead man's waist. He also used the butt of his gun to smash away the rest of the man's face and picked through the mess to find four more balls that the warrior had been holding in his mouth for fast reloading. No lead was to go to waste; all would be needed.

Loading the gun took me some time, and while I was doing this my friend grabbed the back of my arm and gave me instructions that, little did I know, would come to save us.

"Load quickly, boy," he said. "Do not fire until I have reloaded and tell you to fire; follow me if you want to live."

V.

When I had reloaded, Abigail grabbed my hand, and I turned to look at her horrified countenance. I told her we must go, so we took one last look at our cabin – flames and inky smoke licking and rolling through the broken windows – then followed our protector into the woods.

We moved swiftly all night, stopping only twice to refresh ourselves at the streams we crossed. At one of these stops my friend introduced himself.

"I am Sergeant Timms of Hobbs' Rangers. I was en route to find more men to serve my king when I came upon these bloody savages attacking your village. I am going to Fort William Henry to report what has happened here. You may follow and decide what you will do from there."

I thanked him, and then we continued on until the sun began to rise. Sergeant Timms was concerned that we might still be pursued, so he found a good place for us to bed down and instructed us to sleep. He said that he would keep watch. I told him that I thought I should help him. But, the moment I sat upon the soft green moss, my eyelids became heavy and I did not wake until the sun was setting in the west. Timms was shaking us lightly and telling us it was time to go. He gave us a bit of food from his haversack and we washed it down with water from his canteen. As I tipped back his canteen and tasted the water laced with rum, I looked out of the corner of my eye and saw the sergeant staring at my right hand, still clutching the old trade gun. The twilight of reds and oranges colored his stone face and his blue eyes once again pierced mine.

"Alright, laddo. Alright," he murmured in a quiet, low voice.

I questioned him as to his meaning, but his look told me there was nothing else to say. Leading us, he turned and began walking north.

We continued on this way for many days. Each early evening we would rise; I would shake the sleep from my head and help Abigail along. Our pace was fast until we neared the fort. Sergeant Timms explained this was the most dangerous part of returning to a fort because there were always men lurking at the edges, watching and waiting for an opportunity to take some unsuspecting life. He said that he had seen not a few men killed within sight of forts' gates. For the last mile to the fort we skulked from tree to tree, stopping frequently to look and listen for anything that might indicate some enemy's presence. We came to the last few trees before the great clearing that surrounded the fort. Here we stopped and listened very closely. I saw Abigail looking about as intently as Sergeant Timms and I, albeit with a more distant and wider stare. She seemed to try to "feel" for anyone around and then looked to me, giving a skeptical nod; she was unsure. Sergeant Timms caught this look as well and seemed to understand. He told us to wait where we were and then broke cover to run to the gates. Standing guard were two grenadiers. One stood at attention while the other fed a pine knot into a brazier to give some light, but not so much that it impeded their vision. As the sergeant approached, the grenadiers aimed their muskets and shouted a challenge at him. He responded and then they told him to approach slowly, they not removing their aim from him. When they saw that it was indeed him and that he was alone, they allowed him to pass through the man-door in the gate.

Time passed uneasily as we waited for him to return to the door. We waited and kept up our vigil, fearing any moment some savage would come and knock us on our heads. When Sergeant Timms reappeared in the doorway, he had with him a man who seemed a full two feet taller than him. The man looked in our direction to where Timms was pointing. The sergeant then waved at us to come in. I sent Abigail first and tensed, waiting for any movement that was not hers. When I saw her safely duck through the door, I broke my cover and made my way across the clearing. Just as I came from my hiding place I saw another figure appear from farther down the wood-line. It seemed that he had an advantaged angle on me, and I knew that he would get to me before I reached the gates. I ran harder and looked forward to see both the grenadiers level their muskets and take a shot at him. But both missed their target; he was growing larger with every moment. I looked again to see the man with Sergeant Timms drop the pipe from his lips and reach inside the man-door, producing his own musket. My attacker was now only a few yards away. Seeing his spiked tomahawk raised high for a strike, I slid to the ground. I heard musket fire and saw the French man's arm, the one that held the tomahawk, tear from his body in a bloody mess of bone and muscle. He fell to the ground and I pressed the barrel of my trade gun to his head and silenced his screaming. The grenadiers pushed me aside, and I heard a thick Scottish accent exclaim, "Now why did ya' go and do that? We was gonna have a bit of fun wit' 'im."

They dragged his body back to the fort, and I followed them. When I arrived at the sergeant's side he attempted to introduce me to my most recent redeemer.

"This is Solomon," he indicated. "Solomon, Captain Humphrey Hobbs."

The captain did not acknowledge my presence; he seemed more intent upon finding his pipe. He did so and took a pull to find it still lit. The captain then ushered his sergeant through the gates and I came along after.

Inside the fort the grenadiers were ransacking the dead man's clothes, cutting away his shirt and looking for something.

"When yer done with him I want what is left of the scalp," the captain shouted. "That's fifteen pounds I'm not bound to part with."

The sergeant tried to introduce me again but the captain did not turn his gaze from the dead man.

"Sergeant, I heard you the first time," Captain Hobbs said. "You know I haven't much time for savages. Probably not've wasted the lead had I known."

The captain, sergeant, and I continued to watch the grenadiers work over the body. They seemed unmoved by the sight but I shuttered at the thought of what fate might have dealt me.

When the grenadiers finally found a small piece of parchment tucked in the man's sash they handed it to a third grenadier who ran it off to some place in the dark recesses of the fort. The other two returned to their post, and the captain went to the body to begin his grisly work. Just like the sergeant had done in Stockbridge, Hobbs knelt over the body, placing his knee on the head to hold it still. He then swept his blade across the scalp a few time to remove a bit of hair and head. The grisly sound of flesh being separated from bone added to the flurry of pangs that had, in succession, attacked my stomach. When the captain finished he stood and grinned a diabolical smile, the pipe still clenched between his broken teeth.

"Tonight we drink rum, Sergeant Timms," he pronounced.

I felt that I had seen quite enough for one night and turned to the sergeant to ask if I could rest. He led me to the barracks where twenty-five men were in the midst of preparing for sleep, cleaning guns, and smoking pipes. When we walked through the door they all stopped their tasks and stared at me. Some of them grumbled about "dirty Indian" and "putting the savage out with the rest of the dogs," but Sergeant Timms warned them that if any bothered my sister or me that he would deal with him personally. He then barked at them to be "as they were." Later I would discover that most regular soldiers held no respect for rangers and the like, but all knew of Sergeant Timms and, if only out of fear, listened well when he spoke.

I asked where Abigail was and Timms told me that some of the women had taken her off to get cleaned up. No sooner had I asked than she returned in fresh clothing. I ushered her near the fire so that she could warm herself. The sergeant returned with some blankets. As Abigail spread them on the floor near the fire she asked me what the shooting was that she had heard. I knew that she had been through enough, so I told her that it was some men checking their firelocks. She and I wrapped ourselves in the blankets and quietly prayed together, thankful that we had survived our ordeal. We then quickly fell off to sleep.

VI.

That night I dreamt of wolves beckoning me to join them. I was frightened and comforted in the same moment. I crouched in a small stand of saplings, hoping they would not see me. But one came to me and sniffed me warily. Then I fell in step with them; we disappeared into the fog that surrounded us. As I departed I looked back a final time and saw Abigail in the embrace of a beautiful woman – an angel, possibly – with hair the color of blackest night. They were both weeping, but I knew I had to follow, maybe even to lead.

In the morning I woke with a start. Fife and drum announced the new day had come. All around me men were pulling on scarlet regimental coats and grabbing their firelocks from wooden racks on the walls. They filed out the door into the parade grounds. Abigail was still asleep, so I slipped from the blankets and covered her with my half of the bedding. I still clutched the firelock in my hand; through the night I had not removed my recently acquired pouch and horn. I walked from the barracks into the parade grounds; the autumn air did the rest of waking me. I looked down at my clothes; I could see the blood caked on them and feel still more lingering on the back of my neck. All of this certainly lent me a somewhat hideous appearance.

My moccasins, which had dried by the fire, were instantly soaked again as I walked through the dew-drenched lawn down to the end of the barracks to behold the lines of troops. I stood at the edge of the barracks and put the butt of my musket on the ground, leaning the barrel against my shoulder so that I could rub the chill from my hands. The fifes and drums started playing again and I, not knowing what to do, half-hid myself behind the edge of the building. When morning colors and ceremony had been finished and orders were given, I saw Captain Hobbs walking with the fort's headman, Colonel Montgomery, and giving him some report. I looked down the lines of soldiers and saw Sergeant Timms with another man similarly dressed. It was apparent from their soaked moccasins, leggings, and shirttails that they had already been out scouting this morning. I walked from my cover and Sergeant Timms saw me right away. He motioned to Captain Hobbs, who shook his head vigorously. The sergeant spoke more desperately to him, and finally the captain threw up his hands.

"Alright, we shall see," he said.

The three men walked down toward me; each had a look of absolute resolution on his face. The looks took me aback. I shuffled my feet, and when I could no longer bare their gazes I dropped my eyes to look at the ground. The captain walked past me, giving the impression that I was no greater than any other blade of grass upon which he tread. But the sergeant came to me.

"Good day, Solomon," he said. "This is Private Wendell, and together we are Hobbs' Company. Not much of a company, I know, I know, but many of our men were lost to the pox, bloody flux, and a recent ambush. I'm afraid this is all that is left. And that, my friend, is why I have come to speak to you … We have been given orders to go to Boston to seek out new recruits. Prior to that, we will be searching the areas in the western part of Massachusetts Colony for recruits, as well. We need a man who can navigate us."

The captain turned about suddenly and glared back.

"Sergeant Timms, get to it," he barked. "We haven't the day to spend at this task."

"Yes, Your Lordship," Timms replied humbly. "Solomon, we need a man to get us to Pittsfield. Do you know that place and how to get there?"

I knew Pittsfield well. I had been there many times; it was the town just north of Stockbridge, where the men from my village went when they were brought into the British Army. There they procured powder, firelocks, pipes, and other provisions. I told Sergeant Timms this and he asked again if I would lead them there. I asked who would watch over Abigail, and they assured me that she would be well taken care of by Private Wendell's wife.

I knew that I already owed a great debt to Sergeant Timms and the captain, so I agreed. When the captain heard this he wheeled about and came back to me.

"Understand this: you and your sister are now under the care of the British Army. Being under that care you must, in some way, benefit it. There are two ways that a savage can benefit the army. One is to serve your king in the army, and the other is to have your scalp sold."

The second prospect did not sound very pleasant to me, so I agreed to lead these men wherever they needed to go.

The first order of business to prepare me to go with these men was to do away with the old trade musket that I had obtained in Stockbridge. The sergeant took the trade gun and turned it in to the armorer. He then drew for me a new British musket they called the King's Arm. He returned and gave it to me along with some powder, balls, and a haversack full of food provisions. Captain Hobbs explained that all of these things were my responsibility, and if he found that I had lost or misused them he would see to it that I would come to know "the cat." Following my briefing, he had me swear allegiance to the King and gave me a shilling as a token of my sworn duty. Sergeant Timms took the scalp from the man he had slain in my defense and bought a silver ring from the fort sutler. He slipped the ring, which bore a design of two clasped hands, onto the first finger of my right hand – my trigger finger. He said this was the true sign of our new agreement; I thought this fitting, as that finger would best demonstrate my loyalty to the crown.

Captain Hobbs disappeared with the bounty of scalps that had been collected in the few weeks that they had been at Fort William Henry and purchased some other sundries for our journey. These were dealt out so that all shared the load. I eyed my new musket with its shiny barrel and clean brown sling. The wood had a dark, unblemished finish. I then looked at the other men's muskets and decided that there was some resemblance, but it was clear their weapons had not known youth in many years. Captain Hobbs' musket was the same length as mine and was the newest looking of the three rangers'. Private Wendell's musket was also of the same length but looked a great deal more battered. Sergeant Timms' musket was a full six inches shorter. I questioned him about this, but he just grinned and said that it let him get that much the closer to his enemy. I noticed, from looking around, that these men were outfitted much differently from other soldiers. While the regulars wore shoes, three-cornered hats, and bright red coats, the rangers were dressed for the woods. There was little uniform about their clothing. It seemed each man was outfitted as he had seen best for the conditions. Each ranger wore a gray hunting shirt that hung down past his knees; that was the extent of their similarity. I would later hear some talk about uniform, regimental green coats being issued for them – but that was a distant possibility at best, the men assured me.

Captain Hobbs wore a brass gorget, which he complained sounded like a cow bell and swore that he would soon be rid of it. He was the only one fortunate enough to afford shoes. He had a large black cartridge-box slung over his shoulder; it hung down to his hip, beside a huge hunting knife with a deer-antler handle that was tucked in his leather belt. Private Wendell wore moccasins, leather leggings, and a dark blue waistcoat over his hunting shirt. Sergeant Timms also wore moccasins and leather leggings, but of all he seemed the most suited for the woods. He carried a hunting pouch and horn, items not seen among regular soldiers but common to hunters. He had discarded the blue bonnet for a short-brimmed black hat, from which his long blond hair was drawn back into a neat queue tied with a black ribbon. Over his hunting shirt he wore a green waistcoat; this appeared the least aged of his attire.

While the captain was away, the sergeant explained to me my duties as their pilot in the woods. I would move about twenty yards ahead of them and find the trail. I was to be ever watchful for anything that might indicate an enemy presence.

When the captain returned, he found me still looking at my new firelock.

"Don't worry, lad," he said as he slapped me on the back. "She'll be seasoned soon enough."

Of course, he spoke of me as much as he did of the musket. Walking the trail in front of these men would certainly not be the greatest manner in which to ensure a long life. I had heard enough stories to know the pilot's was the most dangerous place to be, and I indicated as much to Sergeant Timms. He laughed.

"Boy, it would be a pity to spend a fistful of years in the woods and then get killed; better the first time yer out," he said.

The men gained great mirth from this, but I found little humor in it and wondered what sort of men these were.

VII.

I spent my first night in the woods with Hobbs' Company in careful reflection. I say "careful" not because I allowed myself to meticulously analyze my situation, but because I had to be careful not to allow my mind to wander as was its habit. Being the new man, I was given first watch. Captain Hobbs dared not risk the safety of his men on a lollard, so he gave me the watch with the least likelihood of falling asleep. But he still swore that if I so much as made a long blink he would see me lashed for endangering his men.

We slept that night on a small point that overlooked a place where three small ravines came together. At the tip of this point was a depression that the sergeant was satisfied would shield our movements. Behind us, the hill rose sharply, making a defined horizon that would give away the approach of anyone trying to sneak up on us. In front of our point and past the ravines was a large lake; it was moonlit, which would clearly show the approach from water and shoreline. I felt relatively safe here. But in time I would learn that this feeling of safety could be a man's greatest enemy, allowing him to be lured from alertness. This night, however, all would remain quiet.

For my watch, I picked a large oak tree that I could lean against while looking over the men. The rangers pulled blankets from their assorted packs; they threw half of these upon the ground. And, after deciding there were no large sticks or rocks that would rub their shoulders or hips, they laid down in one large mass and pulled the rest of the blankets upon themselves.

It was time for me to take my post. Before I crept off, Captain Hobbs whispered yet another warning about the consequences of failure. Then he pulled a captured woolen French stocking cap down over his head.

Darkness fell, and with it the cold night sent its own frigid blanket upon us. I went to my tree and made certain that I could see all around without giving away my own location. I could see the ridge and the shoreline with little impediment, but looking over the edge of the point was impossible because of the slim beams of starlight that broke the canopy. No, this night my ears would have to be my sentries. I realized that a man's eyes can only blindly venture into the darkness so far before they return again into his own mind. In there, I found myself trying to decide how it had come to be that a boy – who, just days before had been seeking game in the calm of the forest – had now become a man squatted behind a tree trying to guard against some awful, violent event. *What do I know about all this?* my internal workings asked. *How can those men sleep? How can they trust a boy to watch over them?*

In all my years of wondering about those men who go off to war, I had reasoned with myself that there was some initiation that transformed their minds, instantly, from unseasoned to iron-willed. I had only heard of how they had taken twenty scalps or outrun a hundred men or charged through a hail of lead. Not once did I suppose that they had ever huddled by a tree wondering if each breath would be their last.

These musings flashed periodically through my mind as it wandered; still I tried to avoid allowing them to wholly consume my thoughts. I knew that just a breath away lay three men that depended on me to call upon every bit of my ancestral ability to keep them alerted to anything of perilous concern.

The timepiece that Captain Hobbs had lent me for my watch caught a solitary moon beam as I shielded its face between my legs. At midnight my watch was finished. I scurried down the slope to rouse Private Wendell. He was startled by my nudge and pinned me soundlessly to the ground, his leathery fists clutched about my throat. But he remembered that I was with them and released his grip while whispering an apology into my ear. This man was a master of the silent. He hardly ever spoke, and he moved noiselessly everywhere he went. He took the small timepiece from me and continued to look over me with watchful glances to assure himself that he had not injured me. I took his place under the blankets at the captain's side and peeked over the edge of the wooly covers to see Wendell stealthily picking his way up the hill to my old tree. My throat ached from his assault, but it reassured me of his strength and gave me that same unreliable sense of security that I would learn to avoid. This assurance, along with the oak-like heat that Captain Hobbs gave off, put me straight to sleep.

The moon was long before setting when the captain gave me a sharp kick to the ribs to wake me. He told us all to get ready to move. I rolled up and tied my blanket with the hemp tumpline and, after assuring myself that the load was riding well, tucked my tomahawk in my sash at my back. Captain Hobbs pointed for me to take the lead. I nodded my reply and made my way to the front of the small column.

I started a quick pace that into which the others fell behind me. My eyes sought out everything – looking, watching, inspecting, expecting. When I crested the hill, I looked back to see the giant moon lingering on the horizon; then I looked forward to see the first rays of the sun burning the dawn sky. I looked again at the moon and saw that it was beginning to be obscured by the storm clouds that I could sense advancing. When first I had risen from sleep I felt the storm coming and its presence reassured my instincts. The clouds made me think of columns of soldiers, and I wondered if the sight of them in the daytime would seem as ominous. Before stepping off again I checked my musket's prime. A bit of evening dew had crept into the pan, so I primed it again.

We walked for an hour before the lofty regiments of clouds released their watery volley on us. No shelter was in sight, and it appeared that there would be none in the near or distant future. So we continued our pace, soaked but steadfast, the locks of our guns tucked neatly under our arms. Near evening we found shelter in the form of a small rock outcropping some ways up a little hill. The sandy floor and deep recess promised a decent night's sleep. The storm had not let up, and it was sure to continue all night; it now added lightning and thunder to its showers. Captain Hobbs scanned the forest, and when he was content that no attack would come that night he gave permission for a small fire to dry our sodden things and warm our tired bones.

Straight away Sergeant Timms, Private Wendell, and I went to work looking for sticks in the cave. When we had produced a small pile, the sergeant drew from his pouch a small tin that contained flint, steel, and charred punky wood. He pinched a bit of this punk between his fingers and flint and struck his steel striker across the flint's sharp edge. Sergeant Timms had mastered this art, and at the first strike the shower of sparks caught on the charred punk. The char glowed as bright as a candle in our shadowy shelter. He dropped the burning ember into a nest of hairy fibers that resembled a bird's nest. Then, he blew steadily upon the hot center; his breath brought fiery life to the nest and it burst into flames. Timms carefully placed this flaming nest on the sandy floor, then he and I cautiously added small slivers of dry wood to fuel it. We continued in this way until the fire was large enough to burn finger-sized sticks, making the whole affair about the size of a good pumpkin. We would repeat this drill for many years to come; it became something of a shared ceremony for us.

The fire produced smoke, and the smoke began to accumulate. Sergeant Timms and I looked at each other and realized we had made a mistake. The heavy air from the rain did nothing to remove the smoke from inside the cave. The smoke began to choke us as we tried frantically to decide what to do. Our solution was to grab a few large logs; we shoved these under the flaming sticks, gathering them and moving the whole affair closer to cave's mouth. The smoke had grown thick; it burned my eyes and lungs as we made our way to the edge of the cave. Most of the fire made it to the entrance, but there was a trail of burning sticks and embers that followed. These we swept toward the main body of the fire with our soaked moccasins. Captain Hobbs was not impressed by our mistake and let us know it with his baleful stare. The small fire gained new life after we had moved it, and soon we were able to strip a few items of clothing and dry them by the warm flames. Private Wendell had disappeared while we were giving the fire life but now returned. I saw one of his drenched arms reach up over the edge of the cave and pull himself into our rock shelter. Under his other arm he carried a bundle of wet sticks which he placed by the fire to dry. With this supply of wood we would have enough to last the night, he reassured.

I pulled my knees to my chest and warmed the bottoms of my feet by the fire. The others gathered around and we ate a bit of food from our haversacks. That night we took turns at watch; the only thing to be seen was the lightning tearing brief, ominous strips from the black nighttime sky.

VIII.

The rain continued, on and off, for days as we trudged toward Pittsfield. We arrived muddy, wet, and tired. The people of Pittsfield were stirred by the recent attacks made by the French and their Indian allies. Many men and women from my village were in Pittsfield. I met with several of my old friends and we questioned each other about the welfare of our respective families. All were happy to hear of Abigail's and my escape. Some related stories of such grotesque savagery that I was made so much the more willing to fight. Most of the men were joining the militia and doing what they could to ensure the continued well-being of their families. Meanwhile, Sergeant Timms was seeking new recruits under the orders of Captain Hobbs. Most men were intent on defending their homes or what was left of them, but the sergeant found two brothers who were willing to enlist with our company. Malachi and Isaac were Pittsfield hunters who provided meat for the village and its small fort. They were unmarried and fine men of the woods. Captain Hobbs and Sergeant Timms were assured of their abilities by listening to tales told by the town's people and were glad to have them join up.

    That evening we found a fine tavern with a generous keep. This man did not hold the same disgust for our kind as was common amongst other. Most believed that it was improper for men to go about the forest fighting like savages. Mr. Coffen, though, understood that our purpose was beyond aimless murder.

Captain Hobbs knew that it would be the last night for awhile that we would enjoy the comforts of an establishment, so he released us to enjoy ourselves. His relaxed state, combined with the keep's generosity, made for the beginnings of a fine evening.

I had tried ale before, but tonight the men of Hobbs' Company were adamant that I partake in rum. This strong drink weakened my mind and released my thoughts. The tavern was crowded with our small rabble, as well as about a dozen other men. A fiddler was playing, and his music, mixed with the rum, gave me the idea that it would be perfectly sensible to coax one of the tavern maids to dance a step or two. I had barely swung her about twice when I felt myself tumbling to the ground. My face hit hard against the earthen floor; I initially supposed that I had tripped in my drunken state. I began to push myself up when a man, straddling me and yelling something about "a dirty red nigger," slammed his fist into my side. The rum had numbed my body, so his strike had little effect but to make me fully aware of what was occurring in that desperate moment.

I turned to face him. He spat in my face while drawing his fist back for another blow. I braced myself and forced my mind to clear. When he lunged, I kicked my leg out and sent him toppling to the floor. Immediately I pounced on him and rammed my knee into his face until I heard the distinct sound of his nose breaking. I stood to give him a few good kicks, but as soon as I was afoot I found myself being dragged back by my hair by another man. I reached for my knife at my waist and freed it while turning my own hair around this attacker's hand. My blade bit deeply into his arm, which made him release his grip and give out a shrill scream. He ran from the tavern with his hand clutched to his wound. His exit alerted Sergeant Timms and Captain Hobbs, who were just outside smoking a pipe and waiting for Private Wendell to return from the privy. The other men in the tavern began to back me into a corner. I stood, my chest heaving ragged breaths, and waited for what might come. But Captain Hobbs entered and grabbed an oak stool from just inside the door. He hurled the stool with such force that it split when it came in contact with the back of the head of one of the men who was cornering me. The others spun around to see where the stool had come from and were met straight away by Sergeant Timms. The sergeant pressed his knife blade to one man's throat and the barrel of his pistol to the forehead of another.

"Ye lads best be on yer way," he warned in a low voice.

Mr. Coffen produced a large Scottish sword and bellowed for all the men to leave save Hobbs' Company. As they scurried past the sergeant and captain, Hobbs put up both his hands and grinned, saying, "That's all the fun you boys will be having with our savage tonight."

When all the others had left, Captain Hobbs walked over to me and looked at the man doubled up on the floor, who was clutching his mangled face, and then at the stream of blood leading out the door. He shook his head and addressed the sergeant.

"A bloody mess, a bloody mess," he said. "But it appears they do raise more than just girls in Stockbridge, Sergeant."

We all laughed, and the laughter rekindled the pain in my side. Captain Hobbs jabbed at my ribs with his finger, saying that I would feel it even more in the morning. He ordered another round of rum. Wendell, Malachi, and Isaac returned, sorry that they had missed the excitement. They all raised their cups in honor of my fight. We threw back our rum; it burned hot all the way from my throat to my afflicted ribs. Finally we set off for much-needed sleep in the generous keep's loft.

We woke early the next morning and made preparations to leave. We walked out of the tavern into the morning light. The light burned my eyes but cleared my head. In the streets were gathered men upset by the evening's events who had come to seek retribution. They looked at our faces and saw that we had no concern for the petty tavern brawl, that we were instead looking for threats of true danger. They backed away and slunk into alleys and side streets as we walked toward the village limits.

At the edge of town, as the main roads dwindled I found a small trail that led in the easterly direction we desired. I looked back at the captain and he nodded his approval. I swept my eyes over the other men. Sergeant Timms was directly behind me, followed by Captain Hobbs. Isaac and Malachi flanked each side. Following behind was Private Wendell. Each man bore a look of absolute confidence and resolve. A small smile parted my lips, and I imagined that the Devil himself could not breach our lines.

I started down the trail, trotting quickly to get ahead of the rest of the men. With the exception of a few linger pangs in my side, I felt good – and ready to face whatever the day might hold.

IX.

We continued through the forest for a fortnight. We slept when we felt a certain amount of safety and moved with the confidence of a pack of wolves. I felt that our presence projected before us and the mere scent of us would drive away any would-be assailants (Though by now I know all too well that this confidence is misleading and can make a man to fall away from his duty of vigilance.). One trail led to the next, and a week after leaving Pittsfield I came across a path that seemed too new to be safe. Our company gathered around Captain Hobbs as I reported my findings to him. He gave us orders to be doubly watchful.

We came upon an old camp a few ridges later. The occupants had built a fire; evidently, they had felt safe. Sergeant Timms and I cautiously entered the campsite while the others flanked out and scouted the edges of the camp to try to determine the identity of those who had stayed there. I found the embers in the pit still warm. Sergeant Timms and I were squatted over the hearth with our firelocks resting across our legs. I looked up to see the others skirting the edges and occasionally bending to pick up something of interest. My eyes swept over them, and as I turned my head a metallic glint caught my gaze. I swiveled my head back in time to see the muzzle of a gun peek out from beside a monstrous oak. I shouted a warning – but not in time. The first shot hit Isaac in the chest; the heavy lead ball caught him mid-stride, dropping him at the base of a tree. Pieces of bone and intestine covered the trunk, and most of his blood seemed to be instantly on the ground all around him.

"Wake up the dead, boys!" Captain Hobbs shouted as he dropped to a knee and returned fire.

I stood momentarily, slack-jawed at what had happened. But Sergeant Timms, always cool, drew me behind a felled log in time to avoid two balls that screamed in, snapping twigs and branches around us. There was movement all about, and I was incapable of finding a target. The fleeting, painted bodies of warriors would appear for only a moment, and then disappear again behind some cover. Isaac was still lying against the tree. He was mumbling something about water, and we watched as Wendell came running toward him, sweeping him up in one arm without breaking stride. The enemy was everywhere – surrounding us, among us. I would see the flash of a warrior covered in red and black, so close that I could smell the bear-grease paint slathered on his body, and then he was gone again. They seemed to be Abenaki, as they wore French waistcoats and conspicuous French crosses around their necks. They also shouted a constant mixture of Abenaki and French words to one another. Captain Hobbs, meanwhile, was shouting orders for us to give Wendell cover. We let fly our shots and then set immediately to reloading, each man firing while his neighbor loaded. With this technique we managed to keep the savages at bay while Wendell slumped himself and his bloody load on the safe side of a large rock. I could see Captain Hobbs leaning over Isaac, cutting away his blood-soaked hunting shirt. A warrior appeared from his cover and ran toward the three, brandishing a wooden war club. Sergeant Timms stood slightly and rolled back on his heels as he took careful aim and slew the painted devil. Isaac, too, was dead. No one saw him take his final breath; most likely he had died shortly after he hit the ground. Captain Hobbs now bent over Isaac's wide-eyed corpse, muttering a quick prayer.

"Heavenly Father, we commit him to your house. Amen," went Hobbs' brief eulogy for Isaac.

Then Hobbs looked our way; his countenance seemed to proclaim that nothing else was to be done. My eyes continued to dart in every direction as shots rang out and balls cracked in close to our few men. Wendell pulled Isaac's horn and pouch from the broken body and slung Isaac's firelock over his shoulder.

"Your Lordship, we best be moving lest we be completely buggered," Timms stated convincingly.

Captain Hobbs nodded, and we commenced to make a hasty retreat. One man would rise, fire, and then run to the rear of our column as the others, with loaded muskets, would hold off any pursuers. In this way, we kept at bay the disorganized savages, who fought independently instead of in unison. This was effective in preventing any further casualties; we kept up our tactical retreat until evening fell and we could no longer be easily tracked. We spent the night pushing hard east and dared not slacken our run for fear of being overwhelmed in the night.

By early light, we came among the first few cabins that marked the outskirts of Boston. One generous fellow gave us quarters and we each contemplated our near demise. Captain Hobbs expressed his outrage at these intruders and their bawdy attempts to attack the English so close to Boston. After resting a bit, Hobbs took account of our remaining numbers, finding Malachi had disappeared in the meanwhile. Before he slipped away he had told Wendell that he was going to avenge the death of his brother and, likely as not, we would see him again. And so we original four set out to enter Boston to replace the pair that we had lost, and hopefully gather more to round out our ranks.

X.

Boston was a sight to behold. I had been there before as a child, but then it had only been for a short time and I had been shielded from the greater part of the town by my grandmother. On that first visit we had to disguise ourselves, as there was a standing law prohibiting Indians from entering the city. In fact, this law still stood when I returned with Hobbs' Company. This time I was to experience all the darkness of the most raucous parts of Boston.

Our task was to find men, and there was no better place to do so than the docks. The townsfolk eyed us suspiciously as we walked down the cobblestone streets. Our time in the woods had given us rough and filthy appearances. Before we had set out from the cabin where we had spent the night, Captain Hobbs had produced a small black hat from his pack and instructed me to wear it to cover my plucked scalp. He also warned me to keep my shirt sleeves rolled down to cover my tattooing and to remove the silver ornamentations that hung from my nose and ears. Hobbs explained that, besides being illegal, Indians were not much liked here and that downplaying my appearance would be to the benefit of my continued existence.

The salty air struck my nose before we crested the last small hill leading to the waterfront. The smell brought back memories of my youth. It had only been a few years, but it seemed like a lifetime ago. I now bore little resemblance to that small boy who had clung to the petticoats of my grandmother.

We walked along the wooden docks that lined the waterfront. A strong stench rising above the salt-sea met me before I saw its origin. Then it appeared: the bound corpse of a man, decaying inside an iron cage. It hung from a ship's yardarm that was planted on the shore. Sergeant Timms explained to me that it was the body of a man who had been charged with piracy. His corpse was left to rot – and to warn all would-be pirates and thieves. Standing uncomfortably close to the thing was a mother who grasped the ear of her small son. She tersely wagged a finger at the boy, no doubt letting him know that the same fate lay in store for him if he did not change his sinful ways. As we continued to watch this scene, a seagull alighted on the cage's iron frame and pecked at the rotting flesh. The sight made my skin crawl and my stomach heave. Finally my thoughts were averted as I heard Captain Hobbs loudly clear his throat. He had climbed atop some boxes stacked on the dock and was preparing to make a speech.

"Ye fine fellows, seamen, traders, and such, come near if you're looking for work," he bellowed. "Many of you have spent a long time at sea, and I offer you reprieve from your constant wandering of the oceans. My men and I seek a few hardy souls to join us in the fight for King and country against the papist bastards who threaten to come into your homes and lay to waste all that has been wrought by fine English hands. I am Captain Hobbs of His Majesty's Army, seeking men of strength to go with me into the woods and destroy the devils where they sleep. So who here amongst you has the nerve to join up?"

His voice boomed up and down the shoreline, gathering a small contingent of all sorts of men. Some slunk off with no interest in such an awful prospect, while others simply staggered over in their drunken state to hear what was being said. One fellow pushed to the front. He grasped in his hand a pint of ale and eyed Captain Hobbs through squinted eyes.

"Ha! Who's this fool who bellows at us like at so many powder monkeys?" the newcomer said to the captain, who still towered atop the crates. "I see an idiot in filthy clothes with nothing to offer but a death in the wilderness."

The others laughed and jeered in affirmation. Sergeant Timms shoved men aside and neared the drunkard, hoping to hush him.

"That'll do man," ordered Hobbs. "Go away, then, if you want none of the King's gold I offer."

"Bugger off!" the drunkard hollered.

Captain Hobbs, now completely angered, began to move down from the boxes to handle this fool who was foiling his attempt to recruit. As Hobbs was watching his footing whilst coming down, the drunk reached down and drew his knife, an item always to be found at the waist of a seaman. Sergeant Timms saw this and acted swifter than could the imbibed man. In one swift motion, Timms drew back the cock of his pistol, leveled it at the man's head, and pulled the trigger. Bone and brain sprayed from the man's face as his body crumpled to the wooden dock. The knife clattererd harmlessly across the planks and into the water. Those who had remained to watch quickly dispersed, and we six were left alone: four from the woods and two dead men, one sprawled with smoke still rising from his head and another in a creaking iron cage. It all had happened so fast, but I had already become accustomed to the swift arrival of death. Sergeant Timms looked at the dead man at his feet, then over his shoulder at the rotting pirate, then back to Captain Hobbs.

"I suppose these won't do. Won't do at all. I wager they can't handle a blade nor firelock the way they are now," Timms said to detract from the hideousness of the moment.

"Yes, sergeant, and I'll wager that these men's fellows won't be running to fill our ranks with our sort of welcoming," Hobbs said, referring to the dispersed crowd.

We chuckled despite the state of affairs we were in.

"We would be most likely to find more help if we were to head away from the direction that mob went," commented Wendell quietly. "There's sure to be one amongst them that will seek revenge despite our legitimacy at killing this fool."

We watched the small group of drunks move away to the north; we then turned and headed south. Shortly we came to the first tavern. It was an ill-constructed shack that appeared to be thrown up with a few scraps left over from an old ship. It was unmistakably built by men of the sea, with planks slapped together and tarred to keep out the weather. Above the door hung a carved sign with a whale being pursued by a small boat filled with men, harpoons at the ready. We were about to duck in when a voice hailed us from behind. The Sergeant swung around briskly, his pistol at the ready. Wendell lowered his musket from shoulder to hip. There stood a man with dark red hair dressed in clothing more suitable to ocean-faring than to land. His hair was twisted in a tight pigtail that draped over one shoulder and was tied at the end with a bit of string; the pigtail was smeared with tar. His shirt was off-white and stained with salt. It was tucked into the ash-colored slops that hung to below his knees. Around his waist was a green sash with a knife tucked into the front. The seaman had black stockings that stretched tight over his muscular sea-legs and ran down into his shoes. The stockings had patches and holes in such a great many places that it appeared little remained of the original cloth. He held his hands out to show that he was not armed, but also showed no sign of fear at looking down the barrels of guns.

"You lookin' for men to join up?" he asked simply.

"What interest do you have in our trade?" shot back Captain Hobbs.

"I've little interest in returning to the sea; had quite enough, really," answered the seaman truthfully.

"All right then, that'll do," stated Captain Hobbs.

As Captain Hobbs continued to interview this newest potential recruit to our ranks, he found out that this man, Whelan, had started out from Cape Cod as a whaler. But two weeks out, his ship had been captured by one of the pirate ships that plagued the coast and he was persuaded into aiding them until he was put ashore. Pirates do not desire to hold company with them that do not wish to be a part of their raids. Unfortunately, it had taken nearly a year for Whelan to be put ashore, during which time he was made to assist the carpenter of the ship as he did not wish to engage in thievery at sea. Ironically, after he had been put ashore, one of the victims of the pirate ship recognized him and Whelan was nearly hung for piracy himself. But a few others came to his aid and vouched for his character. Whelan was not as quiet as Wendell, but nearly so. To be sure, he was an able-bodied seaman but he had grown tired of life at sea and longed to be ashore, away from it all. Most of all, he feared the sea because he could not swim, and the long days and weeks of imagining falling overboard, he stated, had nearly driven him mad.

We were now five and decided to enter the tavern nearby for some much-needed refreshment. We entered beneath the sign portraying the whalers. As we passed under it, Whelan rapped his knuckles against the sign and gave a low chuckle. I was in front of him as our horde entered the tavern, so I heard him say, as he tapped the sign, "None more for me."

The tavern was dark as could be without being entirely shrouded in black. The setting sun sent a few small streaks of orange light through the planks where the tar had crumbled and fallen away. Two long, rough-hewn tables ran nearly the entire length of the single room. Candles crammed into the tops of old bottles spread little pools of light here and there. To one side, a half dozen men sat around a smaller table, listening to one who stood regaling them with his latest story of hunting the whale. The storyteller's face was dimly lit by a couple of candles, nearly burned to nubs, crammed into a tin candle holder tacked to the wall. A sudden burst of laughter erupted from his crowd as he said something humorous; he punctuated his tale with a big wave of his arms that also had the effect of sloshing some of the ale in his cup over his hand and to the floor. This stopped his story for a moment as he, in drunken stupor, turned his bobbing head to look at the effect of the spillage. He made a slight frown and then, without further consideration, launched back into his epic. I was watching all this while Sergeant Timms and Captain Hobbs scanned the rest of the tavern's inhabitants for signs of danger. Seeing no immediate threats, Captain Hobbs fished in his waistcoat for a coin, which he tossed to Sergeant Timms, and ordered up pints for our crew. Hobbs then marched to the corner of the tavern and took a seat at a small table where he could keep his back to the wall and thus have a commanding view of the establishment. Whelan, Wendell, and I joined him, pulling up assorted stools and chairs around the table. Sergeant Timms placed his order and then came to sit in a chair that Private Wendell had procured for him.

"Well, my boys, not a good start here in Boston, but we managed to fool one into coming with us," said Captain Hobbs, "We're in need of finding more, though, before we return to Fort William Henry – or I'll be flogged for dereliction."

Soon, the tavern maid brought our ales to the table. They were contained in well-worn and dented pewter mugs. We relished the ale as we imbibed and soon were on our way to having heads loftily placed in the rafters. The night wore on as Captain Hobbs and Sergeant Timms discussed what our duties would be once we returned to the fort. Our involvement would include scouting for enemies and offering protection to any woodcutters that would be set about their tasks.

Other patrons came and went through the night, but near the end of our sojourn one shifty soul arrived and pulled up, by himself, near a small table in a far corner. When I first saw him the skin on the back of my neck tingled and I watched as Sergeant Timms looked him over. The new man tugged at his tattered waistcoat and seemed to be attempting to secrete his worn shirt, which appeared to be stained darkly, beneath the outer garment. This man was small in height, but his wary eyes missed nothing that occurred in the tavern. Sergeant Timms spied that he was served some cheap, weak grog, and at that decided to approach the mystery figure. Whelan and Wendell were deeply engrossed in conversation, so it was just Captain Hobbs and I left to watch as Timms carefully approached the newcomer. When the sergeant was near, the man's eyes were diverted away and did not see Timms as the sergeant lightly placed his hand on the man's shoulder. The newcomer reacted immediately with a raised, clenched fist as he pulled his arm away from Timms. I could not hear, but saw as the sergeant mouthed the words, "Easy lad."

The man relaxed a bit but kept his guard keen just the same. Sergeant Timms dragged a chair from a neighboring table and seated himself so that he could speak closely with the new man. The sergeant's first act was to beckon the tavern maid, and he ordered the man a proper ale from the coins left over from the captain. I turned to see that this produced a small downturn in the mouth of Captain Hobbs. He quickly replaced it as he looked at me, took a gulp of ale, cocked an eyebrow, and shrugged his shoulders. Timms and the new man conversed for a while, and I nearly forgot about them as I, again with my drink, dissolved into thoughts of my own future. Secure in surroundings and company, my mind wandered to contemplations of where I would be a week from now, a month from now. The thoughts combined with the ale soon made my head heavy, and I was quickly left with the singular question of where I would sleep that night. I was near to resting my head on the table when the door burst open, releasing the bitter sea winds into the tavern and bending the winks of light upon each candle top. Framed in the doorway was an army officer holding a tall pike that he tilted forward to allow its passage through the door. In his other hand he clutched a brightly polished brass and glass lantern. The officer paused for a moment to allow his presence to be known to all that were present. He then strode through the doorway, followed by a dozen red-coated soldiers. He made his way to the end of the tavern and ascended an inclined place in the floor that was regularly reserved for musicians. Captain Hobbs leaned toward me and seethed through clenched teeth, "Major Todd."

I took this to mean that he was a less than desirable fellow and rocked back in my chair to see what would take place. As the tavern began to silence for the major, Sergeant Timms moved to our table with his new acquaintance in tow.

"Gentlemen, your attention for a moment," Todd began. "Tonight a man was killed near here, shot with his own pistol and robbed. I have been sent to capture the vile, scandalous creature that has committed this most wretched deed and demand of all who are here absolute cooperation."

With that, his men began circulating among the men at the tavern, seeking to reveal some evidence of the crime. Major Todd kept his place and swept his gaze over the crowd, soon fixing his stare on Captain Hobbs. The major stepped down, his well-shined shoes clicking upon the wooden floor as he approached our place. Captain Hobbs was quick to his feet, and we responded in kind so that we were all standing when Major Todd arrived.

"Your Lordship. A good evening to you, I trust?" Captain Hobbs greeted.

"Yes. Well, all but this matter with the killing and all. You wouldn't happen to know anything of it, would you, Hobbs?" the major inquired.

"Not a thing, Your Lordship. In fact, we have been here the greater part of the night with nothing to warrant your ire," Hobbs replied.

"You will pardon my inquiry, Captain Hobbs, but the rangers are known to run with not-so-desirable fellows," Major Todd said vehemently. "I see that you have fooled a few into your silly business of woods walking."

Throughout the evening, as the ale had taken over I had made the mistake of rolling up my sleeves, thus displaying the tattoos that adorned my forearms and presenting my identity as an Indian. One soldier stepped forward and grabbed my exposed arm and roughly drew me in near the light of the major's lantern.

"How 'bout this fellow?" spouted the soldier. "A savage, I dare say!"

I was in the process of attempting to free my arm when I heard the distinct clatter of a wooden ramrod leaving a musket. The rammer flashed by my face and creased the neck of the soldier attempting to accost me. The other end of the ramrod was tightly clenched in the hand of Captain Hobbs. The soldier's grip hastily released as he grasped at his afflicted throat. This soldier stumbled backwards and, despite the attempts of his fellow soldiers to catch him, went crashing down on a table. As he only caught the edge, the table gave, catapulting a few mugs and a clay pot across the floor of the tavern; the pots shattered to bits. While I was relieved to be released from the soldier's clutches, I now worried as to what would be the consequence of my deliverance.

"Your Lordship, you will kindly instruct your men to stay clear of mine," the captain declared coolly but defiantly.

The insubordination was not lost on Major Todd, who pressed himself closely to the captain, locking eyes with him.

"Captain Hobbs, you will keep yourself in check. I could have you brought up on charges for this!" the major shouted.

Captain Hobbs never broke his stare and, for what seemed like an eternity, the two stood off and appeared to let pass between them knowledge of past deeds and acts.

"My apologies, sir. You will forgive me, but I have been enjoying the fine Boston ale and have given leave of my senses. It is not often that I, with my men, should enjoy the comforts of a town garrison; I was merely standing in defense of my man. I am accustomed to the law of the forest which, I dare say, is not a familiarity of yours," Hobbs explained in a humorous tone. "You see, we do not allow such breaches in the protection of one another in that environment. It often is the difference between life and death."

Surprisingly, Major Todd let the affront pass and ordered his men to stand down. A sigh passed his lips as he finished his orders. His aloof posture, an attempt to be dismissive, did not match the fear present in his eyes.

"Captain Hobbs, I trust that your stay here will be short and that we will have no further problems from you?" the major half questioned, half ordered.

"We will be gone in the morning; I fear we have gleaned every man hearty enough to take to the woods," Hobbs assured Todd. "Yes, Your Lordship, we will be gone at first light."

"Good, then. I dare say Boston could not take but a few more moments of the smell of rangers in these parts," Major Todd insulted.

Captain Hobbs let it pass; any who knew the true character of men was aware of what had occurred. After one more sweeping gaze of our ranks, Major Todd ordered his men back into the night to search the next tavern. As he pushed through his men to their head he shot back a final decree.

"By morning, Hobbs," Todd bellowed. "Don't have me searching you out on the morrow."

"Not to worry Your Lordship," Captain Hobbs replied. "I think your men would have a time of it once we've reached the woods' edge."

Captain Hobbs made arrangements with the tavern-keep to allow us a room above the tavern for the night. In exchange, we would help him rid the tavern in an hour or so of all its other occupants. While Hobbs was making his arrangements, I listened closely to the conversation of Sergeant Timms and his shadowy companion. Sergeant Timms questioned the man as to if he had anything to do with the murder. The man simply looked at the floor. Timms did not pursue any more information, save to find that his name was Crum. Patrick Crum. Besides the old linen shirt and black waistcoat, he was dressed in ragged breeches with dark green stockings that had seen far better days. When he turned slightly in his chair, I could indeed see a conspicuous dark, wet stain on the shirt. He saw me looking at the stain and I met his eyes – a chilling discovery. They were the most primal-looking devices that I had ever seen set in a man's face. I had seen eyes like that in the face of only one other creature: a bear. I averted my stare and looked off, trying to seem interested in what the captain was to. But I was shaken by the look Crum had given me, and I wondered if he would turn out to be more maniac that asset. The captain wrapped up his affairs with the keep and returned to the table, explaining our accommodations and the conditions of them.

"Whelan, do you know where the naval armorer and sundries are in this port?" Hobbs questioned.

"Yes, Your Lordship. It is down near Red Shield ..." Whelan began, being cut off by a wave of Hobbs' hand.

"Fine, take Wendell and draw two muskets, powder, and shot. If he has any meat stores and bread stores, draw plenty of each. And a few blankets if he has them," Hobbs ordered as he scribbled out the list on a sheet of paper that he had drawn from his waistcoat. "Come back and meet us at the boxes where you were recruited this afternoon."

Whelan and Wendell drained their mugs and ran out the door to their task. The tavern maid set down another large pot of ale at our table. Those of us who remained sat and drank the well-earned beer. Captain Hobbs lit a pipe and for the first time, after a few draws, passed it to Sergeant Timms, who also smoked and passed it in like fashion until it was circling our group in concert with the smoke it produced overhead. This subtle act seemed to bind us in an unspoken covenant.

After a time, we met up with Whelan and Wendell at the boxes. All of us stared at the pile of provision set out. Crum snatched up a musket, snapped open the hammer, and drew back the cock with an expertise that belied his ragged state. Captain Hobbs eyed him suspiciously and asked if he had ever handled one of the King's Arms before. Crum replied with a simple nod. Whelan held his musket and looked down the barrel with an amused look on his face.

"So it's a bit like a small cannon, then, right?" Whelan mused.

Sergeant Timms shook his head, a slight smirk parting his lips. Captain Hobbs turned in disgust. There in the dark hours of night, Timms went through the drill of showing the new men the way to properly load and fire. Whelan listened intently while Crum looked at Timms in brief glances, distracted by other thoughts. When they had finished, Captain Hobbs returned us to the tavern and we scattered the few drunks left in the dankness. We went to our room and Hobbs mounted the single bed while the rest of us jumbled up on the floor, tightly packed in the small quarters.

We were out in front of the tavern before morning's light. The chill of night was still thick in the air. The original four of us had our things slung over our backs. We checked and then rechecked our muskets for anything that would make them not fire properly. The pile of blankets that had been procured the night before lay in the center of our circle. Hobbs looked at them and said that Whelan and Crum would need to find some means to carry them. Whelan looked questioningly at Crum, who did not waste a moment. He disappeared, drawing his knife from his waist as he left our circle. Shortly, he returned with two lengths of rope that looked suspiciously like the mooring lines of a ship.

"Where did you come up with those?" asked Whelan. As the words slipped from his lips a small whale boat drifted by the docks, with frayed mooring lines dragging the water. Captain Hobbs looked at Crum with deep lines crossing his forehead.

"He owed me money," Crum stated plainly.

"Let us get to it before we sound any more alarms," instructed Timms.

"Indeed ..." Hobbs muttered wearily, signaling for us all depart.

XI.

With loose orders from Captain Hobbs and Sergeant Timms, we left Boston, our heavy muskets secure in our cold hands and our new men with their provisions tightly bound over their shoulders with mooring line. The cobbled streets of Boston gave way to dirt roads leading into the hilly country. Soon we left the road and broke into a trail that cut through the forest. We stopped near noon at a small trading post. The trader spoke with Timms and Hobbs at length while the rest of us lounged under a tree eating a few pieces of meat piled on shreds of bread. As I chewed my meal I watched the trader's son, who appeared to be near my age, as he split wood. I could see that he was not working at the same pace as when we had first arrived. He seemed to be leaning to hear the words of Hobbs, Timms, and his father. He slowed and then stopped, resting the ax tip in the splitting stump. He ran the sleeve of his stained shirt across his forehead and looked our way. He was tall but not overly muscular. He had the look of a boy who had lived on the edge of the wilderness his whole life. His long black hair was tied back in a tail with a small piece of leather. He left his work and went to stand behind his father to listen more intently. His father felt his presence and turned, pointing a finger for him to return to the wood pile. I could hear his father, in a thick German accent, telling the boy to get back to his work. The boy lowered his shoulders and began walking back to what appeared to be for him a hated duty.

"On your feet," ordered Timms.

We stuffed the remainder of our bread and meat into our haversacks and I jogged to get up ahead and down the trail. As we were breaking into the woods, I glanced back and saw Crum pull a few apples from the trader's orchard trees, looking around to make sure that Hobbs and Timms did not see his act. Whelan was beside him and began to open his mouth when Crum struck him with the butt of his musket in the small of Whelan's back, effectively closing his mouth. Crum stuffed the apples in the top of his bound blankets and shoved one in Whelan's bed roll to buy his silence. I turned my attention back to my duty and scanned the woods; nothing was there but birds flashing from tree to tree. We moved down the trail at steady pace and were glad to be at our task. The first hints of winter had put a smell in the air, and I knew that it would be a happy occasion to return to the fort and our families. We had continued through the woods about a half of a mile when we heard a horse riding up fast behind us. I looked back; Captain Hobbs ordered us to the cover of trees with a hand signal. We waited and soon saw the trader's son appear on a horse. We broke our cover and circled around him.

"What is it, boy?" Captain Hobbs questioned.

"I want to go with you," said the boy quietly – and a bit urgently.

"Does your father know that you have left him?" asked Timms.

"He doesn't need me," responded the boy. "I've no desire to be at that post forever."

"Your father seemed to say that he needed your help when we were there," offered Timms.

"I've had enough of it," was all the boy could muster. It seemed there was something deeper to his statement which he was not revealing to us.

"I don't think we should be depriving your father of the help that he needs. You'd best be back to him," instructed Hobbs.

A look of humiliated anger crossed the boy's face as Hobbs turned away, motioning us to continue on. I turned to face front, as did the rest of the company, and in the distance I could see a squirrel as it crossed a branch. From where I was standing it was but a speck as it crawled along. Suddenly, the sharp crack of a rifle echoed over us and I saw the squirrel fall. We all turned back to the boy, who was still sitting atop his horse, albeit now with a smoking rifle in his hand. We all turned our heads again, then, to judge the distance of the shot. It was very impressive. Hobbs and Timms consulted in private, and when finished they said that they agreed the boy and his rifle would be an advantage in our ranks. A smile parted the boy's face, and he slung himself down from his horse. He quickly reloaded his short rifle and dragged an oil-cloth haversack down from his horse. With his meager possessions in hand, he gave the horse a light slap on the rump and set it running back toward his father's post. He looked one last time toward his home, as many of us had done before him, and then turned expectantly towards Captain Hobbs.

"Up behind Solomon," Hobbs said, pointing in my direction. He came up and shook my hand.

"Thomas Fehn," he said. We looked down at our clasped hands and he caught sight of my tattoos. I looked back up at him, and he said plainly, "Never had any trouble with them Indians fighting for King George."

I gave him a nod and then looked to Hobbs, who waved his hand down the path in an impatient way. I trotted off again with Fehn in tow and we soon were up ahead of the others.

That night we made camp on a steep slope. I saw Timms eye Crum and Whelan warily as they crunched their apples. It appeared that Timms might make some objection, but before he could speak, Crum thrust an apple into his hand, dissolving his lecture before it started. Fehn was off by himself, so I grabbed my haversack and joined him. Thomas was meticulously looking over the small German rifle. Between rubbing small amounts of grease into the metal of his lock and barrel, he would push a small wedge of cheese or meat from his haversack into his mouth. And so this is how the night found Hobbs' Company as we made our evening preparations.

Soon a small fire was lit and we gathered closely around it to prevent its light from straying beyond our ranks. I looked closely at the faces of each man as he sat in silent contemplation. The older men – Timms, Hobbs, and Wendell – stared intently into the flames, while the newer men seemed to search the shadows for an unseen enemy. Crum, while being new to our ranks, did as the older men were inclined to do, staring at a single log as it intermittently caught fire and then winked out. The older men did not bother to look beyond our flames, because they knew what lay beyond. The smoke gathered in my eyes and I closed them to avoid the irritation, but then found myself in a state of prayer. I thanked the Lord for safe passage, knowing that it would be His will as to when, where, and how He would see fit for me to depart this world. After a short time, our fire was extinguished and we were set to either build our beds or prepare for watch. Fehn was given first watch, and instead of simply finding a place to picket himself to the ground, he chose to climb a giant maple at the height of the hill overlooking our camp. He went nearly twenty feet up the trunk and then, finding a sufficient branch, planted his back against the trunk and began his slow scan of the surrounding area. At third watch I was rousted from sleep and given the Captain's timepiece by Crum. When he first nudged me I must have given out a bit of a cry, for I was greeted with his leathery palm clasped over my mouth.

"Be quiet, damn you," seethed Crum in a nearly inaudible voice.

I slowly walked up the hill and stood at the base of the tree that Fehn had mounted earlier. I decided to stay to the ground. Several hours later I watched the first rays of dawn burn over the edges of the sky. The colors resembled those of the few remaining leaves that clung to the trees around me. I was awed at God's splendor and gave quick thanks for making it through another evening. I remembered a prayer that one of the old men in Stockbridge used to give at daybreak: *Today I will live well.*

I slowly turned my head around to check, again, for any sign of enemies, but there was nothing. I first roused Captain Hobbs, who rubbed his hand over his face and looked at me with a glassy-eyed gaze that bespoke of a deep sleep. He turned his head and then lightly elbowed Sergeant Timms, who snorted and then slowly pressed himself up from his blankets. Soon, everyone was up and once again looking over their bedrolls, readjusting breeches, and situating their hats upon their heads. Finally, we all checked our firelocks and in no time we were once again at the task of pushing toward Fort William Henry.

Along the way we passed through several settlements. Most of the inhabitants were eager to find out any news that might be had. They were appalled by the stories of raids and attacks that had taken place against English settlements, and some could easily relate, as they had been the victims of attacks themselves. None of these small communities could bear to part with any of their men, as these were needed to fill the ranks of their own militias that were forming to deal with the French and Indian threat. At one small village the men were drilling on the commons. Their leader was showing them the finer points of standing in columns and firing in volleys. I caught the sergeant's gaze as we watched. Timms shook his head, muttering about how they would be disappointed when they met the Indians in the woods.

The rolling hills gave way to large mountains as we closed the distance to the fort. Gathering at the base of many of these mountains were small ponds that we stayed well clear of, as water sources seemed to draw the enemy's eye and attention. We gathered our water at any small streams that we came across and made it a point to not linger at their banks. Early winter winds continued to cut through the forest, tearing leaves from branches and scattering them in all directions. The pine trees were beginning to stand out starkly against the burnt oranges and fiery reds of the maple trees' canopies. Getting closer to the fort, the landscape became familiar, which caused us to become anxious to return to our garrison – but also alerted our attention to be wary of enemies lingering nearby. We became aware of more frequent, well-worn trails. I searched each one to try to find signs of recent footprints, but it appeared that most were several days old. Near nightfall of our last day on the trail we began to see newer tracks and our senses were heightened by these findings. The sun had just dipped below the horizon when I saw the first movements of men. I stopped our company, and we laid ourselves tightly to the ground. Sergeant Timms and I crawled to the top of a hill to look down upon those who had gained my attention.

Below us, twenty Huron huddled in a small circle, intent to some kind of council. We watched as they seemed to formulate a plan and then, without notice, broke their circle and began to climb the hill toward where our company was gathered. I looked at the sergeant, who had turned his head and was motioning for the rest of our men to pull up beside us. To me, their footsteps sounded like a thousand deer coming through the leaves despite Hobbs' Company's attempt at a silent skulk. When all the men had made it to the top of the hill and were beside Sergeant Timms and me, Hobbs passed the order, by whisper, for each man to pick his target carefully. The Huron were quickly nearing our place of hiding, and I tried to slow my breathing. When they had come to within ten yards of where we were assembled, Hobbs fired the first shot. It slammed into the closest warrior, who crumbled and began rolling down the hill. The signal given, each man placed a well-aimed shot into a Huron pushing up the hill. Not knowing our numbers or definite location, the remaining warriors began to try to turn from us. The warrior who directed the others' movements, a tall man painted entirely black but for a few small red dots across his face, began yelling at his fellows and urging them toward us. As one they turned, and it was apparent that soon we would be overrun by superior numbers. Now several of us were in different stages of loading and firing: some kneeling, others still pressed closer to the ground. Captain Hobbs, though, was standing and trying to fire carefully while urging us on.

"Put lead in their bellies, men!" Captain Hobbs shouted.

We began to spread out as we sought shelter behind tree and rock from the shots being fired at us. One warrior came fast toward Hobbs. Crum dropped his musket and pulled his tomahawk from his leather belt. He ran down to meet the coming foe and was quickly entangled with the enemy, rolling down and away from us. I did not have time to see where he and the warrior went, as I was intent on holding off the enemy as well as I could. The war captain of the Huron finally began yelling to those of his men that were still standing, and they began to make a hasty retreat as we continued to attempt to pick them off. And then, just as quickly as the skirmish began, the woods were silent again, though the shots of firelocks still rang in my ears. Crum was gone but the others were uninjured. We scanned the woods with our eyes, trying to see if the enemy was attempting to come around us. But it was soon apparent that they had fled. Hobbs gathered us near a tree. He ordered that none of us sleep and that each keep vigilant watch throughout the night. This order was not hard to adhere to, as each of us was certain that the Huron would return in the night with a thousand warriors to finish us. At daybreak, with no enemy around, we began to search for Crum. We found him near the base of the hill, where he had come to rest with the warrior that he had been engaged with. The warrior lay at his feet, his throat cut. Crum did not look much better. His shoulder was flayed open, and blood oozed from the gash. He appeared to be barely conscious as we came to him. Whelan and Wendell each grabbed him by a shoulder to lift him. Wendell, who had grabbed him near the wound, was greeted by a deep grunt and a hateful look from Crum.

"Can you walk?" Hobbs questioned.

"Yes, I'm fine," was Crum's unconvincing reply.

Crum was placed beside Whelan, who carried his firelock and helped him when he began to stumble. Each time that Whelan tried to lend assistance, though, Crum shook him off and mumbled a few salty curses.

As noon neared, we came within the area controlled by Fort William Henry. We crossed the open ground with little concern for the enemy, as there was a large force of regular troops out drilling near where we appeared from the forest. As we broke the tree line, Sergeant Timms shouted for some of the soldiers to come help our wounded man. Crum's head shot up proudly and declared, "No, I'm damn near…"

Then Crum fell forward with no apparent attempt to catch himself. Several soldiers roughly gathered him up and rushed him into the fort. There he was brought into the small cabin that housed the fort's surgeon-barber. Crum was laid out on a table and the surgeon pulled off Crum's shirt, exposing the deep, meaty wound. Around the cut the skin had turned dark red and purple. The surgeon used damp cloths to wipe away the crusty blood and pus that gathered near the wound. Captain Hobbs, Sergeant Timms, and I stood nearby, waiting to hear what the surgeon would say about Crum's injury.

"I suppose that I will need to cut the arm off so as to save him," declared the surgeon.

"Damn," was all the captain could say as he ushered Timms outside.

I stood over Crum, who had fallen unconscious, for a while and was soon met by Abigail, who came and hugged me and wept a few tears of joy at my safe return. She pushed me from her and held me at arm's length to study my face. I felt like a son who had overstayed an evening excursion and was now coming home to receive my scolding. Abigail continued to hold my shoulders as she turned her face to look at the bloody mess that was Patrick.

"Who is he?" she asked.

"He's one of the newest men to join up with our devilish rabble," I said, not without a grin.

Abigail slowly turned her gaze on me again, and this time her brown eyes had gone hard with anger. She held me in this manner until I felt compelled to look away.

"Solomon, what has happened to you? Where is my sweet brother who left this place just a few short weeks ago?" she wailed. "I can see in your face that you have changed too much. What have they filled your head with? You are not considering staying in the company of these men, are you? I…"

But her words were cut short by tears welling up again.

"Sister, you cannot possibly understand what I have undergone in these few days," I said in a voice and manner common to a warrior. "They have seemed more like years than weeks, and I have found in these men the brothers I never had. It is certain that they would batter down the gates of Hell for me – and I for them."

"You are a boy! You are my brother! I will not lose you over this meaningless squabble between the white men for land and gold," Abigail shouted this decree as I continued to look away. "Your mind used to be filled with thoughts of prayer, the quiet of the woods, and a green-eyed girl. Now your thoughts are consumed by hate and war and killing. Be sure that you will not win this battle, even if you kill all of your enemy; I have seen it in many faces while you were gone. I have heard their talk and have seen their ways – making ready to fight and consuming the landscape and the trees and the animals as they prepare their killing campaign.

"Do you want to be this man, Solomon? Look! Look at what happens!" Abigail screamed as she pulled at the destroyed shoulder of Crum, producing a small grunt from his unconscious depths.

I could say nothing. I tried to embrace Abigail to let her know that all would be well, but she would not allow it. She buried her face in her hands as her body shook with tremors and sobs. I cleared my quickly choking throat but could think of no words that would bring her comfort. The surgeon returned with an evil-looking saw and an assortment of rusted knives. He began to set up for his grisly work. Abigail looked up from her hands with tears cutting through the small red painted circles that adorned her cheeks. She watched with wide-eyed horror as the surgeon began to set up for his cut, and then she pulled his arm away from Crum's body.

"Stop. Stop this," Abigail said in soft but assured voice. "I will fix it. I can take care of his arm."

The surgeon looked at her with disbelief. He began to disregard her but she stopped him again.

"Please, sir, I have seen such things and worse," she stated. "I can make this heal."

The surgeon looked at the wound and then leaned forward to smell it.

"It has not turned to festering yet and it is relatively free of maggots and corruption," he said. "I will give you a day to see what you can do with your witchery, and then I must do what is ordered of me."

Abigail looked at me with red-rimmed eyes and asked if I could go look for some of the plants that she and I had gathered on other such occasions – she ever-prepared to set aside her own state of affairs to provide comfort for another.

"Boneset, heal-ale, and some moss from the base of the pine trees, Solomon," she instructed. "And get some willow to help with the pain."

I went to gather these things. I knew well where to find them, as I had been taught so by my sister. My senses were still raw from the chastising I had received from her, and I spent the gathering-time plunged in a deep pit of contemplation. When I had brought in the items sought, Abigail went to work making a poultice that she knew to draw out the fire of the wound and make it heal.

Over the next few days she continued to ward away the surgeon as she dutifully repaired Crum's injury, bringing him slowly back to wakefulness.

XII.

The season plunged on, and soon the nights could not be bared without a few blankets. I continued to assist the rest of Hobbs' Company as they stood to their duties at Fort William Henry. Crum returned to our ranks in the span of a fortnight but was unable to go on a scout until a month and a half had passed. We spent several late fall weeks giving security to wood-cutters as they laid up enough logs for our winter's stay. In that time we saw little sign of the enemy except for the occasional warrior, no doubt sent to spy on our fort. Our company, in addition to other rangers, was sent to scatter these men and to disrupt, as best we could, their activity.

One morning, while standing guard for the cutters, I smelled the first true gusts of winter. The scent clung to the inside of my nose; I can explain it only as the smell of *cold*. The final harvest was taking place, and it nearly felt like I was home again. My comfortable thoughts were usually stolen from me by the sight of soldiers drilling or other rangers standing near me; in such moments Abigail's admonitions always returned to haunt me.

With the last of the crops brought in, a night was set aside to have a celebration. It is a night that still shines brightly in my memory. The fifers and drummers started the festivities with a roll and play. The hard-worked soldiers enjoyed this revelry with much delight. Some danced, their arms linked together in furious displays of footwork. Following the fifes and drums, the Highlanders put on their own show by playing their bagpipes, much to the dismay of Captain Hobbs, who detested pipes' shrill wails. One Highlander threw upon the ground two swords arranged to form a cross. He danced in the spaces between the blades, and Sergeant Timms explained that this ancient dance was done by Highlanders before they go into battle. He said that they attempt to not touch the blades, as they take this as a sign of bad fortune in war. It was an excellent display and reminded me deeply of some of our old war dances. The Highlander held one hand on his hip and another high in air above him, and his kilt leapt with him on each jump. He managed to miss the large basket-hilted swords, and at the dance's end was greeted by cheering and rough play from his fellow Scotsmen. All the while during the music and dance, we enjoyed pints of ale and a lovely concoction of cider and rum, warmed in a kettle by the fort brewer. Officers could be seen circulating among their like with bottles of French wine that had been captured during the summer raids. When the Highlanders had completed their show, the large gathering of the fort occupants broke apart into small groups that huddled around small fires near their respective camps.

Hobbs' Company was no exception; in fact, we had the most bawdy and cheerful of camps. Private Crum returned to our fire, after being absent for some of the Highland display, with a fiddle that he had acquired. His return with the instrument brought raised eyebrows from Hobbs and Timms, but they did not inquire as to where he had attained such a rare thing or what he was to do with it. He tucked the small object to his hip and drew the bow over the strings, producing a small screeching that made the lot of us to cringe. He pulled the fiddle away and turned the small knobs on the neck this way and that until he was satisfied. The fiddle finally tuned, Crum struck into a furious melody that soon had many of us leaping about the fire and spinning those near us in a lovely splendor of dancing and laughing. Crum continued to play, and other rangers who did not have the privilege of such fine music began to gather near our fire, making our circle quite large indeed. Soon our camp came to include not only rangers, but regular troops and officers, as well. Patrick played songs that some men knew and sang along with. I had learned some of these songs, and soon Sergeant Timms and I had planted ourselves on a log across from one another and, while Crum rested, we traded song for song while others joined in the choruses. As the fire burned down, so, too, did the gaiety of our tunes. Crum sang an ancient tune that spoke of warriors gathering together in some secret place and rising in great fury against their enemy. It was all quite stirring.

And so his songs continued in this somber way. Old Irish war songs – and no finer to display them than Crum, who remained a great mystery to us. Some information was starting to be revealed, but still we knew little about him. It was speculated that possibly he had been a regular soldier in some little-known campaign. It was evident that he was very accomplished with a firelock; and now there was this revelation of fiddle-playing. He was obviously educated – even worldly in some aspects that befuddled officers that he came across. Still, Crum let on little about his past.

One aspect of him that he was having trouble concealing, though, was his interest in Abigail. They had come to be well acquainted while she administered to his wounds. As our songs began to slow in pace that night, I watched across the dim flames as he took her hand and drew her close to him to dance. To finish the night, I sang a final song that dealt with men forging into a dark early fog, hearing their enemies' horses and experiencing the final moments before dashing into a certain death. These words were not lightly taken by my audience, men of war themselves. Each of us was set once again to remember our own station and our own path. I felt regretful at song's end for killing the jovial mood, but I was assured it was a fine song that needed singing.

Strangely enough, it was Captain Hobbs who told me this as he placed a solemn hand on my shoulder. I did not expect words such as this from him, but rather from Sergeant Timms, as I had come to find him more aware of such sentiments. But Timms was not to be seen at song's end. Whelan said that he had seen him walking away near the end of my singing, pint tucked in one hand and an unlit pipe in the other.

Our circle now broke apart. Many could be seen drawing themselves – and their silent contemplations – away from the flames. Patrick and Abigail drifted away. I saw, as they slipped from the last of the light, him tenderly wrapping an arm around her waist – the very arm that she had saved. I, too, was thinking of my own song as I pulled a small pipe from my pouch and pinched a bit of tobacco in its bowl. I led myself away to where several soldiers were standing guard, and watched them from the shadows. They saw me as well. These few knew of me and did not mind me, though I knew that many other soldiers would be uneasy at the thought of a "savage" overlooking their work. Of these others, I knew, not a few would jump at the opportunity to "mistake" me for an enemy warrior and dispatch me as such.

As the night deepened, I wandered the camps, skirting the outside perimeter of the fort where the various ranger companies were stationed. Some continued their festivities until the new day's sun burned on the horizon. I continued to ambulate and imbibe many strong drinks throughout the night. Finally exhausted, I came upon a secluded place where I threw down my matchcoat to catch a brief moment of sleep before dawn's light. As I drowned drowsily in the evening's dying darkness, my mind swirled toward thoughts of home – and thoughts of her.

XIII.

Early morning found me encrusted: a late fall frost clung stubbornly to my matchcoat. During the night I had drawn the garment over my head to hold out the chill. I listened, from underneath it, to the early sounds of the day: men with their ever-present coughs, birds flitting and chirping, metal cups clanging against stone, breath being blown harshly to awaken old embers, and the lowing of the fort's cattle. These great beasts were the source of a humdrum but constant hazard at night; all feared they might roam from their pasture and trample us in our sleep – a minor fear, all things considered to others, but a nonetheless unpleasant way to meet one's end. I pulled down my cover and saw Patrick, fiddle clutched to his chest, quickly and silently stalking off to return the instrument to the unsuspecting owner. When he returned a short time later he spotted me lying awake on the ground, and he gave me a spry wink and a wide grin.

At that moment Captain Hobbs ducked out of the small hut that we called our home. He rubbed a single rough hand over his face and blinked a few times as he watched the early light burning away the morning fog. He then poked his head into the hut; his voice echoed in the hollow as he urged the other men to fall out for our morning scout. He looked around, apparently searching the area for me, and then he looked over as Patrick pointed out my location.

"All right then, boy, over here with you," he barked at me.

Captain Hobbs began by recounting the events that had transpired and the signs that we had discovered over the last few days of scouting. He reminded us that there had been an increasing amount of enemy tracks in the hills along the northwest of the fort and that we should be doubly aware of anything out of the ordinary.

"It's my belief that the river vermin will take one last heavy shot at us before the snow is deep," the captain asserted.

With the conclusion of our morning's orders, Captain Hobbs, with Sergeant Timms in tow, walked the length of our ranks inspecting our firelocks, knives, and shot pouches, making sure all was in order. Fehn had forgotten to draw more lead after the hunt he had gone on with several other rangers from another company. For Fehn's infraction he was given an extra watch for that night and told that any further misconduct would draw stiffer punishment.

The morning scout went without incident; the enemy signs that we came across were the same ones we had encountered before. The moccasin and shoe tracks had begun to fade in the wind and rain; nothing new was found that might alarm us. Thus went Captain Hobbs' prediction of one final raid before the onset of winter: It faded, unfulfilled, into autumn's end.

During the winter, the blacksmith's dog bore several pups, and I adopted the smallest of them. She was skinny and shaking when I brought her to our hut; most of the other men questioned her ability to continue much longer in life. But she lived on and grew. Namoosh was a great comfort in the long winter nights as she huddled close by my side.

Most of our company's time was spent making musket balls and patching moccasins. And gambling – when, that is, the captain was not around, as he staunchly prohibited the vice. In February, our routine was punctuated when a Huron scout was captured while he was trying to reconnoiter our fort. He knew little, but that little was beaten and prodded from him as best as could be done. He said that the French were gathering at Carillon and at Niagara. It seemed that the French would be making a push to capture and hold all of the Ohio Territory. This put the officers in a great fury; they blazed through a thousand possible battle scenes, attempting to forge plans and contingencies.

This commotion affected us little in our small hut as we weathered out the winter storms, except when we were forced to listen to Captain Hobbs' complaints about the stupidity of this and that officer. However, as a result of the news brought in by the captured warrior, we were sent on more scouts to try to attempt to gain more knowledge of our enemies' movements. Many times we came dangerously close to an enemy encampment, and some nights we were forced to remain in the woods. When nights like this befell us, we would all gather beneath a tree and sit with our backs to it, encircling its trunk with our bodies, our muskets pointing out like the spokes of a wagon wheel from Hell. These nights were desperately frigid, and I would often spend a great part of the night simply praying for the sun to rise so that it would warm us a little. I often wondered if the chattering of my teeth would give away our location, but I was fortunate to never draw the attention of any enemy. The variance in how men bore these temperatures and weather was extreme. Whelan, accustomed to life on a ship that could quickly outrun frigid gales, fared the worst; several times I saw him warming his feet on the belly of a fellow ranger willing to share his heat. Captain Hobbs and Fehn did well with the conditions and were quite possibly the only ones who ever caught moments of sleep during those nighttime forays. The sensation of the cold creeping into every part of my body is unexplainable in its desperate totality, except to say that it felt as if death itself was visiting my body while I was still fully lucid and forced to experience every grinding moment of what was occurring.

When we embarked upon these winter scouts, we strapped to our feet the large wooden snowshoes provide to us at the fort. These wooden hoops laced with rawhide helped to prevent us from falling deeply into the drifts. It was only obvious just how well the snowshoes aided our procession when we attempted to do any walking outside of the fort without them. While keeping us from falling through the snow, they were quite cumbersome to run in; not a few times we found ourselves toppling down a hill when the snowshoes' back stakes crossed and pinned our feet to the ground while the rest of our bodies continued forward. We encountered another disadvantage when entering and leaving steep valleys or gorges; when part of the shoes jutted over the open air, they would nearly splinter under our undistributed weight. Thus, we were forced to crawl on hands and knees in and out of the valleys.

Other times, when we were made to cross large parts of frozen ground, we strapped devices called ice-creepers to the bottoms of our feet. These evil contraptions, with small metal bands that rode under the arches of our feet and two vicious-looking spikes that bit into the frozen ground, were so uncomfortable when wearing moccasins that I soon "forgot" where I had placed my set.

As I have said, despite our occasional forays into enemy territory, nothing of great importance occurred that winter, and we were mainly left alone by the marauders from the North.

XIV.

As winter came to a close, the approaching spring was heralded by the groans and cracks of Lake George's ice. Sometimes the blasting sounds that emanated from the lake brought alarm to the fort's inhabitants, as the sounds imitated musket fire with startling perfection. The warmer times also brought about contests of gun play. No wagers were made, as gambling was forbidden, but each contestant knew that he offered up his honor as a trophy. No man was as handy with a musket as Sergeant Timms, who consistently placed ball after ball into the center of any target. Patrick abstained from the games and was content stealing or borrowing books as opportunities arose. His thirst for knowledge was insatiable and Captain Hobbs, through other officers, attempted to assist Crum in his scholarly pursuits.

My attempts in the marksmanship contests were met with varied results. I was not a perfect shot but was assured by Timms that my skill was solid enough. He also stated that when these games are being played, little thought is given to how matters change when the target is shooting back. Fehn was disqualified from competing against the regular soldiers and rangers, who bore muskets, because of his German rifle that could never miss. But Fehn was seen sneaking off to contest some of the hunters who laid about the fort when they were not in the woods at their trade. These matches were known to the officers but were conveniently looked upon with a blind eye, as the hunters had helped to provide desperately needed food stores in the long winter months when the fort had drawn tight the rations.

Sometimes Fehn would return from his impromptu matches with a new bearskin or bundle of beaver pelts that he quickly traded away for coin that went to provide welcome ale to his fellow rangers. Some of the wealth that Fehn accumulated was given over to Captain Hobbs, who procured two short blunderbusses that he and the sergeant assured us would be well-used assets in the coming spring campaign. Both blunderbusses were fitted with hemp straps that Abigail wove. Timms placed one of them under his care; the other went to Fehn, who carried it on his back as a good accompaniment to his deadly rifle. While Abigail was busy creating these straps, I worked at creating a new bow to replace the one that I had lost during the fight in Stockbridge a season before. The fort blacksmith created two dozen finely balanced arrowheads for the willow shafts that I had rendered and soon I, like Timms and Fehn, had an additional weapon to assist in our duties.

The warmer winds brought a small sloop to Fort William Henry. The ship was loaded with fresh recruits to assist the troops already garrisoned at the fort. Included were several men who were brought into our company. Their names included Porter, Lockridge, Lowman, and Wheeler. Wendell, who was older than any other man in our ranks, had become enfeebled from the winter treks; he was released to assist the fort's gunsmith. His departure was met with sadness, and his quiet demeanor and quick wit were sorely missed by our men. But little could we afford to fixate on this loss, as so much time was needed to assist the newest members of Hobbs' Company. Outside the palisades of Fort William Henry, Sergeant Timms and Captain Hobbs were busy showing us the finer points of the King's Service. Our scouts became more intense as spring rose about us. We knew that the French would be sending their own men out to reconnoiter our situation, and we meant to capture or kill them before they could return to their homes.

As morning broke one day in mid-April, we were called to a special duty. We were splayed out inside the fort during morning parade when we heard shots being fired from outside the fort walls. Presently, Captain Hobbs had been administering a tongue lashing to Lockridge for being imbibed at this early hour. Hobbs had given him this same warning before, and now lashings would meet Lockridge's continued infractions. But the company's collective attention was drawn from this spectacle as the low thud of musket fire rolled over us. Captain Hobbs looked to Colonel Montgomery, who gave a look of confusion in return.

"Captain Hobbs, have any of the men been sent to the hunt or to game at this hour?" Montgomery inquired.

"None of mine," Hobbs replied.

"Then you shall send your men out to discover the meaning of this disturbance," Montgomery ordered.

"At once, Your Lordship! Hobbs' Company – join up and prepare!" Hobbs shouted. "Prime and load, and damn you if you not mind your hammer stall."

Quickly then we were out the gates of the fort. We could see a large barn burning down near the lake. Warriors rushed about about. I set out hard down the hillside with Crum and Fehn close behind. Timms fell in line twenty yards behind us, with Captain Hobbs not far behind him. To Sergeant Timms' left was Whelan and to his right was Wheeler. Lowman, Lockridge, and Porter fell in, flanking and covering the area behind Captain Hobbs. The area between us and the small farm was cleared of trees and shrubs. Several of the enemy took up shelter behind a small boulder that sat on the lakeshore and began firing at us as we approached. The sound of balls snapping and whistling past and about us was ever present as we rushed to close the gap. Behind me I heard the distinct roll of drums and the shrill call of fifes as the regular troops were being brought in line inside the fort.

As we continued to run toward the burning farm, I witnessed a scene I shall never forget: A burning man, trying to escape the inferno of his home, was kicked in the chest by a savage the instant he emerged outside. The man continued to struggle even as he was engulfed in flames. He writhed and crawled about on the ground, finally hauling himself to his knees. But the moment he did so, the same savage who had kicked him dispatched him with a swift strike to the head with a large war club. The warrior then stretched to his toes to give out a scream of triumph, but he was cut short when he fell into the sights of Fehn's rifle. The effect of this warrior's death was immediate. His companions all flinched as if they themselves had received the fatal shot. That their comrade had been felled at such a great distance disturbed them; they began moving away to the forest with their ransacked items and one small boy in tow. Captain Hobbs called a stop to our pursuit, but I looked to Crum. He had also seen the boy, so he and I carried on in our run. Captain Hobbs again gave out his order.

"Hobbs' Company, back to me!" he called.

I slid on my heels and yelled back to him, "Captain, they have a boy!"

Hobbs held his hand above his eyes to shield them from the morning sun. He scanned the escaping war party and then locked his gaze on the man struggling with a flailing and kicking little boy. Without hesitation he gave out a new order

"Get up there, Solomon!" he shouted. "Crum and Fehn – go with him! The rest of you with me!"

The war party had pulled ahead of us by quite a bit and was leading its captive into a small ravine that ran from the lakeshore and along the distant edge of the fort's clearing. Crum, Fehn, and I sped toward a small crest that led parallel to the ravine, and we raced along it as best we could. Patrick and I edged along the ridge, with Fehn watching the back of our trail to reassure that we were not cut off from the fort. So far we had been unseen. We reached a point of the ridge that looked down into the ravine. The warriors must have thought we had broken chase, for they had slowed down to better secure their little prisoner. We watched as three men attempted to tie a cord onto the hands of the small boy. The boy was unrelenting in his struggle; his teeth flashed out like those of a crazed animal, biting and nipping at the hands trying to hold him. Likewise, he kicked his small feet at every part of the men's bodies that came within range. It was far too dangerous for Crum and I to fire on the warriors for fear that we might strike the child; but suddenly he broke the grip of the most recent man to snatch hold of him and struck up the side of a tree with startling speed. Before long he had made it to a perch fifteen feet in the air above the men's heads. One warrior started to point his musket up at the boy, but his muzzle was slapped away by the man I supposed was the war captain.

Now that the boy was clear of the war party, Patrick and I worked quickly. We made our plan carefully. We were greatly outnumbered but supposed that, with surprise and speed, we might gather up the boy and get away before too much attention was drawn toward our rescue attempt. Fehn drew up between Crum and me, laying the barrel of his short rifle across my shoulder to steady his aim. His shot brought down the war captain and made the others spin on their heels to see where the attack had come from. They were met by Crum and me rushing shoulder to shoulder down the hill, giving up the most frightening of war screams. As two of the enemy squared themselves to us we fired our muskets and they dropped to the ground, each shot through the chest. Upon firing, Crum and I split apart and the remaining warriors were met by Fehn, who had taken the blunderbuss from his shoulder. He let fly with a massive load of lead shot, scattering all those nearby. We could hear more warriors crashing through the woods toward us, and we made quick work with our tomahawks and musket butts of the wounded enemies. A great flood of painted devils was nearly on us when firing from their rear produced more death for them; the rest of Hobbs' Company had arrived. Looking through the trees to the war party's rear I could see Hobbs bellowing orders to Sergeant Timms and the others, who were working the King's Arm as best as they could to put down the warriors. Now, wedged between the two parts of Hobbs' Company, the enemy warriors had nowhere to hide. They forgot about the boy and their pillaged goods so as to merely save their souls. Soon, those warriors who had not been killed were running hard away from the fight; we kept up our fire until the last of them were dispersed.

When it was clear that they would not return, we all gathered underneath the tree that held the small boy. Captain Hobbs yelled at him to come down, but he would only shake his head. Tears streaked his trembling, soot-covered face, a moving sight to several of us standing below. Patrick handed me his musket and began climbing the tree toward the boy. At first, the boy began to scream, but the soothing words that Crum spoke as he approached him eventually calmed him down. Soon, Crum was up with the boy, holding him in his arms and reassuring him that he was well and that he would be protected.

Slowly, Patrick climbed down the tree with the boy clinging to his back. They reached the ground safely, and Captain Hobbs went over to take a look at the boy. He reached out his hand to pat the child on the head, but the boy bit him ferociously. Hobbs drew back to strike the boy, but was stopped by the look in Crum's eyes that suggested he would deliver a vicious reprisal if the boy were met with another injury. The captain simply backed away, rubbing his injured hand. Patrick cradled the boy in his arms and carried him back to the fort. At the gates we were met by many of the soldiers and inhabitants, crowding about to witness our return. At the head of the mass was Abigail who, upon seeing that we were unharmed, wiped tears from her eyes and modestly but briskly walked to meet Patrick and me. Namoosh was there as well; she came to me and diligently licked a small wound on the back of my hand, giving up a small whimper of concern. I scratched her behind her ears and soon all were able to take a breath of relief.

In the days following the raid we would be sent out many times to reassure that there were no more rovers about our fort. All had a sense that this was the beginning of a long summer season of raids, defenses, and bitter death.

XV.

If Abigail and Patrick had been close before, the boy's arrival into their lives sealed their relationship. Abigail still held all sorts of reservations about the work that we did, but she also understood the importance of it if any in the King's colonies were to ever enjoy a semblance of peace again. The bond between Patrick and Abigail was a true testimony to love surmounting seemingly impossible odds. Soon they decided that they would be wed and Captain Hobbs, who in his small village had served as a deacon, performed the marriage. It was another fine time for all who attended. Upon forming their union, they immediately brought the little boy into their small family. While his Christian name was Abraham, most called him by the Indian name that I had bestowed: Hannick, or Squirrel, after his fateful escape up the tree on the day of his delivery from the devils' hands. It was astonishing how much like Patrick Hannick appeared, despite not being his true son. The lack of a blood bond seemed to have no effect on the relationship between these two, and Patrick could not be seen without a small shadow following behind.

As my peoples' tradition prescribed, I was charged with the education of my nephew. I soon found that Hannick possessed a natural ability in the woods. I once took him on a walk through the forest; shortly upon embarking, I snapped a small twig beneath my foot. Hannick, being my "scout," turned and held a small finger to his lips, indicating I should exercise greater care in my patrolling. It was difficult for me to stifle laughter, but the look of amusement was drawn quickly from my face by Hannick, who saw my smirk and presented me with a look of stern displeasure identical to that often brandished by his father. It mattered not to me that Hannick was not born of Patrick and Abigail's mingled blood; he was their son as much as any who ever lived. And he had become my nephew without question.

The new spring brought the birth of other relationships. Most notable were the fine ladies that Sergeant Timms and Whelan gained. These ladies were sisters who came to the fort to work as wash maidens. The women who worked in the fort were not of the same dainty stock that was often seen in the East. They worked as hard as any man and, if not for them, I am certain that the fort would not have functioned with any success. Sergeant Timms' lady was named Hannah. She was of a Virginia family that had moved near the Ohio Valley until all – save her and her sister – were killed in a raid by Shawnee warriors. She and Sarah had been captured and lived with the Indians for a great while. They escaped a few years after their capture; having no one else to whom to return, they had slowly made their way to this place, serving as laundresses in many of the British outposts along the way. Both were good-natured and had gained many backwoods skills in the time that they had lived with the Shawnee.

Abigail enjoyed having at hand women with knowledge and skills akin to her own, and the trio spent a good bit of time relating various tales and woodland remedies to one another. Unlike Sarah, who preferred not to dwell on the sisters' captivity, Hannah had adopted and retained many Indian traits. She displayed these openly, and she often referred to herself by her Indian name – Tamusquis, or Muskrat. The company of these ladies made a fine addition to our group. Whelan and Sarah were an amazing match, as amazing as ever had been seen. It was not long after the sisters' arrival at the fort that these two found each other and became fast companions. As word passed down that our company's departure was growing nearer, the two were married following a short courting. Sergeant Timms and Hannah chose not to become wed but were no less close than the other couples. Captain Hobbs made occasional utterances about those "living in sin," but such views were dismissed by the Sergeant, who chose his own path in matters outside of his military duties. In actuality, it seemed that Hannah pursued Sergeant Timms with greater diligence than what was reciprocated, he seeming to weigh matters of war greater than those of romance. Regardless, the unions that were formed in the early part of that year brought immense joy to all of us brothers and sisters involved.

XVI.

Preparations at the fort accelerated; we had received word that the army would be marching west. Our scouts continued to return with information that the French and their allies were drawing in supplies and otherwise making ready for their summer attacks. The English were no less consumed in our own preparations. War loomed on the horizon.

In anticipation of our army's march, Captain Hobbs dispatched small parties of our company to range into the wilderness. In one instance, Patrick, Thomas Fehn, and I were ordered to go as far west as we safely could in a week's time, in order to see to the path upon which we would lead the hat-men in their march against the French. I took advantage of this shared time in the woods to get to know these brothers more deeply. In those few hours in which we were not bent upon stealthy silence, we gathered our few souls together in conversation. As he grew more comfortable with us, Patrick revealed more about his past. In particular, he spoke of one campaign upon which he had been sent – a campaign to attack the Fortress of Louisbourg, located far to the north in the papist lands of New France. I had never seen such things as he described, and was enthralled as he sketched upon our imaginations the immenseness of this fort. He assured us that it was like nothing constructed in these lower colonies. As they drew near the fort, the soldiers captured a large island in the harbor, an island protected by Louisbourg's giant bastions. The island battery, he explained, was larger than most forts in the rest of the colonies. The attack went well, as the island battery was lightly defended. Patrick shook his head as he placed the final touch on this tale:

"We would have taken the fort with much less incident if not for some drunken bastard who, upon our capture of the battery, yelled out 'Hizzah!' and betrayed our secrecy. His cry brought about a hideous volley from the fort's guns. All was nearly lost, but we were able to press on and capture the fort itself. Some French officers attempted to escape in a small sloop, and our officers were at a loss as to how to impede the vessel until, as usually occurs, a few of us dirty men took the initiative. We grounded our muskets and swam to the sloop with our hatchets. There, we boarded the vessel and took the papist girls as they sipped their wine. Unfortunately for them, there were no officers amongst us to yell quarter for them, and they all fell to our sharp blades. Solomon, you would have been proud of the lovely scalps I took that foggy night. We gathered what was of value to us and burned the damn sloop. Not long after, I was tried for the murder of French officers. I was in need of a quick escape from the North. Those officers think that this whole business should be prettier than it is. And when we few who dare to deal out the most hellish punishment to those who oppose us go about our work, we are branded killers and unjust. Damn them."

Patrick finished this tale with a note of soft fury, and I, for one, was left with little to say on the matter. I only knew that I was most gracious to Divinity that this devil was gathered together with me and mine.

"You know, Solomon, that story is not unlike the circumstances that presented themselves in Boston, when I joined in with Hobbs' Company," Patrick added.

He looked at me with eyes that chilled my bones, and I nodded at him to continue.

"That night a rich man, with heavy pockets, would not spare me a single coin – not one pence so that I could eat. He left me with a curse and turned down an alley, I followed him with the thought of simply persuading him to generosity, but he jerked a pistol from his waistcoat, and I grabbed for it in the dark. Due to all the danger and turmoil in which I have found myself, it was in my nature to turn that muzzle away – and as I did, he fired, killing himself. He was one of the few I have killed that I truly felt was an unnecessary death. Just one damn coin and he would have gone home; damn his lack of generosity and surplus of pride ..."

Crum finished his revelations, and Fehn and I allowed his words to fall over and envelop us; truly, Crum was wise beyond his years.

Suddenly, a movement in the trees brought us about, and we laid out in silence to see to the commotion. It was a small deer. As we had been out many days and our food stores were low, I drew and arrow and strung my bow. There I brought down the little doe, and we kindled a small flame to cook and dry the meat. Before I had dressed out the meat, I thanked God for our food and the deer for its sacrifice. The latter part of my blessing was looked upon with curiosity by the others, but also with an ancient understanding that welled up from places they had forgotten lived within them. I placed the head of the deer so that it faced home, knowing this would encourage future deer to give themselves up for our sustenance. We finished drying the meat, then we packed it and struck our camp. The stories of Crum fell over me once again and became part of my spirit.

From then on, if ever I saw a needy hand when I held a shilling, I gave of some.

XVII.

We returned to Fort William Henry with news that there would be many small streams and creeks to ford as the army made its way west. Other than the occasional old camp, we had come across little that would indicate we would be impeded as we made our way. Furthermore, our Iroquois brethren had assured our safe passage through their lands.

On our first morning after returning to the fort, we finished our morning scout early and were dismissed to attend to our own needs as we saw fit. I crawled to the top of the fort's bastions and watched as the evening's stars were slowly obliterated by the ceaseless columns of light sent forth by the sun. I thought of Abigail and Patrick, which brought a small parting of my lips. And then my lonely life came to find me. Thoughts of *her* raided my mind, and I was unable to force them out; though, truthfully, I didn't really want to. The sensations always passed through in generally the same manner. First, something to tease back a memory – it usually did not take much. Perhaps a smell akin to the scent of her hair. Then the memory would fully develop; it would always start with the eyes, and then the rest of her face would appear. Abigail was right; Catherine was my smile when I could muster no other happiness. The worst part of the memories was their parting – they dissolved suddenly and apparition-like. And I would find myself alone, wondering where and how she was. It was amazing – and sometimes, in my darkest moments, vexing – how such a short period of actual events could occupy so much of my thoughts, and for so long.

By now the sun was creeping over the horizon and I knew that I should rejoin my company. I hopped down and crossed the parade ground, glancing one last time over my shoulder toward the eastern sky and casting the memories' remnants from my mind. Fortuitously, I soon came across a childhood friend – Noah Oakum – who bore news of Stockbridge. Rebuilding had begun, and the men of Stockbridge seemed to be making a name for them and their like. Apparently, the raid on our village had awakened some profound fortitude, buried deep beneath the years we had spent peacefully in the embrace of the Church. When the French and their allies planned a raid in the North, Noah recounted, warriors sought always to pass as far to the west or east of our village as possible – for, they whispered nervously, the Mohican Wolves had torn their fetters asunder and had been unleashed.

Nonetheless, in preparation for any who might make an attempt on Stockbridge, Reverend Jonathan Edwards had seen to a small stockade being erected near his mission house. As I listened intently, Noah told me about the small ranger company he was scouting for and their abundant ignorance. I told Noah that I had fared better than he, having been fortunate enough to take up with a group of fine men. He assured me that my luck had always been such. Then, with a pained look, he questioned me about Catherine's whereabouts. My look told him enough. He averted his eyes and we silently contemplated the early morning light; his inquiry had sent my mind on yet another fruitless errand. Noah and I were drawn from our morning meditations by the sudden rattle of drums.

"Looks like another company of hat men coming in," Noah stated.

"Looks like," I said with a nod.

Two columns of crimson-clad soldiers marched briskly though the fort's gates. Leading the columns was an officer perched upon a white stallion. Even from the distance that separated us, I could see his gold braids and crisp three-cornered hat. He also wore a gorget about his neck – the ever-present, ever-clanking mark of a British officer. Captain Hobbs had surmised long ago that gorgets were not conducive to an extended life in the forest and had duly cast his aside.

"Scout! You – Noah!" called the sergeant of Noah's company. I realized that Hobbs must have been looking for me by then.

"God be with you, Solomon," Noah said. "Find me when we start west."

"I'll do that," I returned. "God speed, Noah."

By now the new company was completely through the gate and I thought that on my way back to my company I would skim by and take a look at these fellows. I jogged to catch up with them and then kept pace alongside. The first few soldiers I encountered sneered or chuckled at the sight of me. I ignored them, knowing one day they would be happy to have me out there scouting the wilderness in front of them. Most of them would probably never know the grief that I might save them nor what comforts they were afforded at rangers' expense. I found one fellow, though, who did seem contemplative, so I began the usual line of questioning I employed with new arrivals.

"Where are you marching from?" I inquired.

"Boston. We just came into port a month ago, and straight away they have us crossing all of the King's Land. Hell of a ride across the Atlantic. Thought for sure I'd be tossed over; quite a few, quite a few," he rambled.

The man spoke like no one had ever turned a willful ear his way. He continued on about storms, rats, black drinking water, and wormy hard tack. I listened intently to what he had to say until the shadow of a mounted man fell across the talkative soldier's face.

"Pray tell your worry, private?" came from above.

That voice. I knew that voice. I spun around and came face to leg with the British officer. As I looked up I could see, in the breaking daylight, the face of the very same major with whom we had clashed in the Boston tavern.

"Do you seek something in particular, scout, or just to bother my soldier?" he spat.

Despite my attempts to remain unresponsive, I glared up at him and shook my head. I realized that he did not recognize me and I thought it the better. So I made off toward the head of the columns. Along the way, I re-primed my firelock and thought about what we might be sent against today. My pace was quick, and I overtook the soldiers one by one, as I knew the Captain would certainly be looking for me by then. I reached the head of the columns and turned my head for a glance at the major's lady, who had accompanied her man to this distant place. I wondered what sort of person kept company with his like. She was looking hard right – away from me – as I approached, but as I closed the last few feet she looked straight ahead. My damn head felt like I had been struck with club.

For there, riding upon a horse at the head of the columns, as though she had materialized from my recent, melancholy musings, was Catherine. Catherine, my Catherine – now the woman – the lover – of Major Todd.

"Did she see you?" Abigail asked a short while later.

"No," I shot back sullenly. "She was looking ahead. I saw her as I ran beside the columns."

"Why is she with the Major?" continued Abigail.

"I do not know. Did you suppose that I would speak to her? I have not seen her in years. She probably would not even recognize me," I sputtered in frustration.

"Are you sure it was her?" Abigail asked in a very sisterly fashion. I responded with a glare.

"Hobbs' Company, fall in!" came the captain's order.

I rushed out to join up with the rest of Hobbs' men. Crum ribbed me with his elbow when I fell in with my fellows.

"Where have you been?" he asked

"In hell," I replied curtly. Crum looked at me in confusion as we neared the columns assembled on the parade ground.

"Present your firelocks!"

The order was sent down by captains, sergeants, and corporals, echoing throughout and above the massed men. In unison, each firelock was briskly brought up so that the bottom of its stock rested near the knee of each soldier. The muzzles of the guns were canted up and at an angle. The English colors were paraded down before us and back. "God Save the King" was played on fife and drum while men remained with their firelocks presented – all a fine show by the new company. At the conclusion of the ceremony, that which I dreaded most occurred. Colonel Montgomery came to review the troops and as he rode past, Major Todd fell in beside him – with his lady close behind. By now, some of the newer men had begun to shake, as they were not accustomed to standing at present for a long duration. The more seasoned men, however, endured this drill passively.

My eyes shifted to the mounted officers riding down the line. Thankfully, the officers had rid themselves of the notion that Indian scouts should stand at attention and no longer required it of us. Still, we were expected to be silent and to not turn our backs on the colors or officers. The reviewers' approach made me anxious, and I began to unconsciously shift from foot to foot. Captain Hobbs noticed my uncomfortable movements and whispered for me to settle. Unfortunately, the captain whispered his words just as Colonel Montgomery and his fellow riders came abreast of Hobbs' Company. Colonel Montgomery, ever-watchful and ever-hearing, caught Captain Hobbs speaking and knew that he must address this infraction.

"Captain Hobbs, is there something the matter with your scout?" inquired Montgomery

"Your Lordship, I believe he is anxious for the wooded trail, to seek out England's most hated enemies," Hobbs replied. "You are acquainted with how these savages misbehave and must constantly be reined to their duties. Your pardon, please, sir."

"Hobbs, send forward your scout," Montgomery ordered as soon as Hobbs had finished his groveling. In that moment I felt as if hot lead were being ladled into my ears and scalding metal being pressed to my face. I obeyed, stepping from my place behind Hobbs' Company and presenting myself before Colonel Montgomery. I stood with my eyes cast down and my musket hanging limply at my side.

"Major Todd, this is one of our red Indian scouts," Montgomery offered instructively. "Note them well; they are worthless at standing guard or procuring water or the many other menial tasks we set our soldiers to, as they consider such duties 'women's work.' But their knowledge and skill of the forest is unsurpassed and invaluable to our quest against France and her papist king."

"Yes, Your Lordship, I will bear this in mind the next time that I encounter one of these dogs sniffing near my men," Todd replied. This was greeted by a sideways glance and a turn in the saddle by Colonel Montgomery.

"Pray tell, have you been the receiver of some mischief by these fellows?" Montgomery questioned.

"Lordship, just this day when we were arriving, I found this particular scout – though I must admit they all look quite the same, but as I believe it, this one – questioning one of my men of his march from Boston," Todd replied. "With all due respect, sir, you should be careful of these fellows, as they might set out with such information and hand it to the enemy for nothing more than a jug of rum."

Major Todd nearly glowed as he gave forth what he surmised in his own fiendish mind to be the truth behind the motives of my fellow scouts and me. This angered me greatly, as I supposed myself more properly in place and competent at this station in the wilderness than he would ever be. I tightly clenched my musket in my hand until Sergeant Timms quietly blew through his teeth at me, a sound imperceptible by any except one accustomed to listening constantly for harbingers of danger signaled by little more than a chirp or click by those brothers stalking behind him. Silence fell over those looming above me; the major and colonel were obviously waiting to see if I would make some bold retort. When a few moments had passed and still I had said nothing, it was clear that Colonel Montgomery was truly mulling over the words – say I, the lies – spoken by Todd. Colonel Montgomery edged his horse near me. I could smell the sweat of the beast and I was incorporated into a swarm of flies, the likes of which accompany these creatures at all times.

"Scout, what is your name?" inquired Montgomery.

My heart crashed into my stomach.

"Solomon," I muttered lowly, still looking at the ground and the hooves of Montgomery's horse.

"Scout, when I ask you a direct question, you will look at me and give me a direct and clear answer," Montgomery nearly shouted in his thick Scottish accent. "Now, out with your name!"

The moment was inevitable. I slowly lifted my head up to direct my gaze at Colonel Montgomery's ruddy face, bulging eyes, and tightly drawn lips. In the corner of my vision was a blurred image of Catherine, who was looking toward me, though not at me, with eyes squinting in the streaming morning light. Her face seemed to show little concern for the goings on.

"Your Lordship, I am Solomon of the Stockbridge Indians, scout for Captain Humphrey Hobbs' Company of Rangers," I stated in a loud, clear voice.

I continued to hold his gaze, but from the corner of my eye I could now see that Catherine, over the colonel's shoulder, was adjusting forward in her saddle. At the mention of Stockbridge she had brought a gloved hand to her forehead to shield the sun; and this is how she was now to be found, staring across the void, looking at a ghost. Catherine's face was twisted in confusion and what I might have taken for anger had I not remembered that this was the look she took when concentrating deeply.

"That is all, scout. Return to your position and mind you be more attentive to officers," Montgomery ordered.

My eyes shifted for a moment to Catherine, and then I quickly withdrew myself and moved to stand behind Hobbs' Company once again. I felt her eyes upon me as I moved. The sound of horse tails swishing resounded like thunder in my ears as I began to make my turn. I came back around to face forward and watched the procession of three mounts continue on. Catherine, her chin tucked tightly to her shoulder, half-turned her face toward me. Seeing me returning her look, she brought her head back around and I could feel other eyes upon me. Sergeant Timms had not missed the exchange of glances, and he now wore a shining, humorous countenance upon his face; thankfully, he spoke no words.

Finally, all were dismissed, and I immediately made my way toward our ranger hut. I felt hurried steps falling behind me, but I would not look back. Then a hand came gently to my shoulder, which caused me to stop and turn. Sergeant Timms was standing there and he still retained his look of amusement.

"Solomon, Scourge of the French, Taker of Scalps, Walker of the Night's Edge, have you, with all these accomplishments, also lost your damn mind?" Sergeant Timms laced through his laughter.

I shook his hand off of my shoulder and tried to press on.

"Oh, Solomon, come now! Be truthful and do not tell me lies," Timms insisted. "That cannot be the one that you speak of; surely you have made some confusion. May be that you swallowed too much powder during that last little scrap we were in and it has eaten your brains, is that it?"

The sergeant kidded on. I, too, was now unable to keep from laughing, and Timms greeted this by running up and tackling me to the ground where we fell in a heap of firelocks, pouches, and wild laughter. Captain Hobbs came upon us and inquired as to what we were doing. I noticed that as he questioned us, his words were followed by a sharp coughing fit that rattled his entire body and left him doubled over, his fist to his mouth.

"Captain, are you all right?" Sergeant Timms inquired.

"It's nothing ... just the dust all these damn men have been kicking up," Hobbs explained away. "What with all the many new ones here, I can't hardly walk anywhere without getting a mouthful of earth in my lungs. You men meet up with the rest of us at the hut; we need to go over the morrow duties, as we will be escorting a group of boatmen when they carry their bateaus to the lake's edge."

With that Hobbs walked away and left Sergeant Timms and me sitting side by side on the grassy parade grounds. We stared at Captain Hobbs as he walked away, and Sergeant Timms remarked that he believed the captain had borne this cough for a few days now, and that it had grown successively more severe.

"He's also a little pale, I should think …" Timms said somberly. "… but not as pale as you were when you saw Major Todd's lady!" He ended with a piercing whisper, then pushed on my chest, thumping me back against the ground.

He continued to laugh as he braced his musket against the ground and hauled himself to his feet. Wiping away tears with the back of his hand, he stood over me and gave me a beaming grin. Then he grew more serious.

"She is the major's woman and you should be careful, Solomon," Timms said slowly. "But war is a hellish place, and from the words that I have heard spoken about the fort, what we will soon be set against will be like nothing you have ever seen – and the likes of which I have encountered but briefly. So, brother, if there is something that you need to say to her, do it quietly and do not bring notice to yourself. It is likely we, as rangers, will be sent into the very Devil's maw. So I say to you from experience, do not leave words unsaid."

Timms offered nothing more, save that same stare I had first seen back in Stockbridge. He then removed himself from my view, leaving only the endless blue sky before me. I closed my eyes for a moment to drink in his counsel.

But soon I was returned to the present when Patrick roughly dragged me to my feet.

"Damn it, Solomon, we haven't the time for sleeping," he said. "I swear to Christ you'd nap on the battle line if there was no protest. Let's go!"

And go we went, as I followed him in a slow jog back to Hobbs' Company's encampment.

XVIII.

I had imagined that my reunion with Catherine would have been very different, but here we were: far from home and in a wild and distant place in which neither of us had ever supposed we would find ourselves. I tried to fool myself into thinking it possible she had not thought it me, but knew this to be an untruth. She had recognized me.

I wandered the fort and saw to my duties as always but was left with the haunting realization that I would need to speak to her when the opportunity presented itself. We were being desperately set at the many tasks needing to be performed for the march. One aspect that created difficulty was that Captain Hobbs' sickness had worsened and Sergeant Timms was left to many of the duties normally reserved for a captain's charge. Abigail attempted to create succor for Hobbs, but nothing seemed to relieve the great pains that visited him, and his soft coughing had turned into a hellish bark that shook the whole of his body when he was set to the fits of his illness. This caused a distraction to us, even when we were not in his presence, as we each saw him as a great leader and friend. The day came when Captain Hobbs could no longer raise himself from his pallet, and we were all acquainted with the realization of what path our captain was on.

On the day prior to his death, Captain Hobbs was blessed with a few moments of lucidity. He called us all to his bed and we stood, encircling his broken body. A strong spirit still burned from him as he slowly turned his head in a final review of his soldiers.

"Men, I am short of this world and will soon be home with my Father," he began. "You all know well your duties, and I trust that you will be true to them and to your king."

His benediction was interrupted by a horrible, rasping cough that visibly caused him great pains – pains which bolted out amongst us, buffeting the lot of us in waves of shared misery.

"You will continue on and be good men; leave no path not ventured, leave nothing unsaid that you mean." This last was said as his slit eyes fell upon me, he echoing Timms' words. Then his eyes turned to Timms himself.

"Sergeant," he said, his voice nearing a whisper, "the company is yours."

He finished with another coughing spell and we excused ourselves from the hut as Abigail and the other ladies attended to his pains. In the night, Captain Hobbs' life passed from him and he was prepared for burial. No man, despite his strength and spirit, was capable of keeping back the tears that burned hot on his cheeks. With hideous disbelief, we were made to lower this great man into his final place. Before we placed Captain Hobbs into his grave, Sergeant Timms stepped forward with a eulogy to him.

"Your Lordship, we have fought bravely beside you and now stand ready at this final place where you will, one day, rise to glory to meet our Creator in the sky," Timms began. "Great God in Heaven, watch over our captain and friend. Sir, we shall meet you in Heaven, where there will be no more partings – no more partings forever."

This said, each man grasped the thick leather straps that had been placed underneath Captain Hobbs' body. He had been bound in his white, wool blanket that was emblazoned with a giant *GR* and the British broad arrow. We bent our backs as we slowly lowered his heavy body to the earthen depths. Another company volunteered to replace the soil, and we went away, separating from one another as we drifted. I walked a few paces from Hobbs' grave and braced myself against a tree. Whelan came to me. He placed a gentle arm around my shoulder and drew me near. He explained that he had lost many brothers at sea and that it never becomes easy, this business of past friends. His words were comforting and made the dealing easier.

"Solomon, you know how when we come to camp that we stack our muskets together so that they all stand and all hold each other up?" Whelan asked. I nodded. "That is like this – we each will hold each other up, alright?"

His words, although forming a perfect consolation to my first loss of a dear friend, brought forth more tears, at which Whelan drew me closer and assured me that this is the way of things. I hated it. I was still young and did not want to come to such fates. My thoughts were lost in the idea that a man who had stood so strong in the face of our enemy could be stolen away by something such as this. Were we not all meant to die a great death in battle? I began to understand, not without bitterness and regret, that not all events in life are as a man might imagine or hope them to be. Thanking Whelan for his words, I shuffled away. Soon I caught sight of a figure, draped in a dark cloak, standing on a nearby knoll. I drew the rough cloth of my shirt across my face to brush away my grief and then looked longer at the cloaked person.

I knew that it was Catherine but was unsure if I would approach her. Major Todd had not attended Hobbs' burial, as he had thought Hobbs an adversary and had held great disdain for him. My face clear, I steeled myself and walked toward Catherine. She was standing alone. As I drew near her, the gray sky broke with a light rain that fell upon everything. When I gained her position, I viewed her face, enshrined in the hood of her cloak. She bore a dark countenance, and the sight of my renewed tears brought forth from her a likewise state.

I wanted to embrace her but could not bring myself to it. I sat down at her feet as we lamented the death of great Hobbs – my tears for my friend and hers' for me. I sat so near as to feel the fringes of her cloak against my back. Some of the highland men who had benefitted from the presence of Hobbs' Company approached Captain Hobbs' grave. Despite his avowed, vocal disagreement with the sounds of bagpipes, he always seemed also to hold a secret reverence for them. Now, as the highlanders played their dirge, the sounds did little to distract me from my grief; truly, they made me to weep more deeply for our lost friend. The light rain began to fall stronger and Catherine pressed herself near me, looming overhead to shield me from the downpour, offering what comfort she could to me. No words were exchanged as we mourned all that had passed in a few years. But we were not to remain long in this state.

"Catherine!" a voice called shrilly. "Woman, there you are? What is this? Damn you, what are you about? I told you not to come to this thing. Why do you cry for this sad bastard? And why are you near this savage?"

Major Todd's curses continued as Catherine backed away from me and faced him. I was still set in my place and would not acknowledge this usurper's presence.

"Wife, return to quarters this minute," Todd ordered, then turned his voice upon me. "And boy – I will have words with you."

I heard her go. I also heard Todd's footfalls as he neared me. My anguish was suddenly replaced by rage as my soaked shirt, which had started me to shiver, clung to my body. My shivers of cold were changed to tremors of anger when the Major grabbed my arm and tried to haul me to my feet. I slipped and staggered on the wet grass as I was spun around to meet the jealous husband's face.

"What the hell do you suppose you are doing drawing near my wife, boy?" Todd yelled.

Lightning had now begun to cross the sky, and I stood facing a man that I absolutely disdained for a thousand reasons. I was repulsed by his disgrace to my fallen captain and I was sickened by his relationship with the one whom I so loved.

"Scout, I will take your life if you so much as glance at my wife, do you understand me?" Major Todd threatened.

He continued in this manner, gradually escalating his vows of injury. I would not bring a fight in this place of sacred rest for Captain Hobbs, so I allowed him to continue his threats so long as he did not make a move to cause real injury. I supposed that I would probably kill him on this very ground if he pressed the issue, but when he could elicit no response from me save a blank stare he made his final comment about me being a coward and then stomped away, following Catherine's trail and yelling after her. Major Todd's words trailed off as he sloshed back to his comfortable place in the fort. A strange duplicity rose in my mind as I thought on these two officers. Captain Hobb had come to accept and embrace me. He had been fair and honest while Major Todd embodied everything that I abhorred. I pushed thoughts of Todd away as I paid my final respects to the man who had led us through the most arduous of tasks. The rain had by now soaked me so thoroughly that my very bones ached. I walked to the grave and pulled an arrow from my quiver. In a sign of honor I drove it down into the moist earth, as deep as the fletching. I stepped away and said a silent prayer.

My return to the ranger hut was met by Wendell, who had returned for the wake. He pushed a clay mug that was filled with ale into my hand. I quaffed down the beer and slid the cup across the single rough table that stood in our cabin. Instantly it was refilled and handed back to me. All raised mugs gave celebration to our captain and his deeds. Patrick had regained the fiddle that he had procured earlier and began a slow reel that was so like that one which I had heard, long ago, on the banks of the Housatonic River.

Too many memories, thoughts, and emotions swept over me in those moments and I felt near insane with the bombardment. Those long hours wiled on as we imbibed deeply. Songs were sung, *huzzahs* were placed on a passing soul, and every few moments were broken by this or that man or woman's cries and sobs. No laughter echoed in our cabin that night, and the next morning we were excused from our duties. Our sorrow knew no boundaries.

A final note on this evening is that sometime when the rain subsided, Sergeant Timms drew us all out of the hut and had us fire a volley of honor – and it is truly amazing that no one was injured, as we were all by that hour unfit to handle a musket.

XIX.

Near midday after Captain Hobbs' funeral, we rose and boiled hot water for use in making tea and for cleaning our muskets. Few words were exchanged as we sat in a small circle, exchanging cleaning rags and mugs of hot beverage. The rains had gone but the skies stayed gray. A messenger was sent from Colonel Montgomery requesting Sergeant Timms to present himself to the major's office. Sergeant Timms rose and drew a musket ball from a small pouch hanging at his belt. He cut a patch of cloth from an oiled strip hanging from his pouch strap. He used this to gently wrap the huge musket ball, and then he squeezed the ball in his hand. Bringing his powder horn to his lips, he pulled the small plug with his teeth and shook a small bit of powder into the pan of his musket, snapping closed the hammer and drawing the cock halfway back. He dumped more powder down the musket barrel and then used his thumb to push the patch and ball into the barrel. He did all of this with practiced precision and watched us rather than his hands as he drew the ramrod and pushed the ball down, seating it properly. His face held no expression as he jammed the ball, bouncing the rammer a few times and then replacing it against the musket barrel. We had all stopped our cleaning, and a few still sipped teas in silence as we watched him.

"Crum, watch the boys while I'm gone," Timms said. "Make sure they all clean their guns, and send two men to draw lead and powder. Send two more to fill the haversacks and ask the ladies to finish the washing. Solomon, with me."

And so passed Timms' orders, just as we had received them so many times before from Captain Hobbs. I drew my matchcoat over my shoulder and loaded my musket as we walked.

"Right then. You bastards off your arses and quit your dallying," Crum ordered as we left.

Sergeant Timms and I walked through the gates of the fort and crossed the parade ground to Colonel Montgomery's quarters. He and I stood shoulder to shoulder in the doorway as we looked in. Montgomery was obscured by several officers who were leaning over a table and discussing battle plans, their pointed fingers running here and there over a map. Timms looked over at me but said nothing, and then looked back into the office. One officer straightened himself and rubbed a hand in the small of his back, eliciting a popping sound from his spine. He turned and we saw that it was Major Todd. A fiendish grin spread across his face as he looked at us standing there and my blood ran cold.

"Sergeant Timms. Come in, come in," beckoned Montgomery. "Leave your scout at the door."

Timms looked at me again, and I turned and placed my back against the wall next to the doorway, listening.

"Sergeant, my condolences at the loss of Captain Hobbs. He was great man and his service will be missed," Montgomery stated. I heard a small puff of air dealt out, no doubt, from Todd. "Sergeant, I will be elevating you to lieutenant in the absence of Captain Hobbs. It was initially thought that you would accompany the force that will be going north, but I have decided to attach you to a light infantry company that will be passing to Schenectady to push west. You will be with Major Todd's company and I trust that you two have been acquainted?"

"Yes, Your Lordship," Timms and Todd answered in unison.

"Good then," Montgomery said. "Major, explain to Lieutenant Timms what he is to do to prepare, and be sure that he and his men are properly provisioned as you will be leaving on the morrow."

"Lieutenant, have your men draw lead and food ..." began the major.

"Already done, Your Lordship," Timms said through clenched teeth – I knew this even without looking.

"Do not interrupt me, man! I am your superior, and you will see it as such and address me as such. Do you understand, lieutenant?" Major Todd's voice rose to a girlish squeal in his indignation.

"Your pardon, sir," gave Timms.

"Now. Return to your godforsaken hut and be ready for morning formation. Do not allow your men to get drunk this evening, as we will be pushing hard to gain Schenectady in a few days. Are my orders clear enough for you, ranger?" Major Todd shouted, injecting derisive laughter in the words *hut* and *ranger*.

"Splendidly, sir," Timms returned. I heard the swish of his coat as he brushed against the table, turning to go.

"Stop!" Major Todd squealed again. I heard Timms pause. "Now, then, you are free to go; dismissed," Todd gleefully gave out.

Sergeant Timms burst out of the doorway without even looking my direction. His steps were quick and heavy.

"Scout," Timms growled.

I had to jog to catch up to him, and when I did I could hear him muttering every curse and disparagement that he could think of upon Major Todd's head.

"That son of a whore, bastard, ass of a mule..." Timms continued. At one point he stopped and turned to me.

"You know, I was fighting the French before that yellow bastard even thought of strapping on a sword," he uttered. "While he was sipping his fine clarets and eating fruit from the islands, I was scraping ticks off my legs with a knife, eating whatever we could find that wasn't too rotten, and getting shot at every time we crested a hill. That monkey's arse couldn't find his way through the forest if a straight path was cut a mile wide to where he was going and now, *now* we are supposed to be attached to his company and traverse hundreds of miles to God knows where! What more shit can be piled on us?" Timms exploded in great rant.

"Well, congratulations on making Lieutenant," I said optimistically, which nearly elicited an injury from Timms. He really did growl then, and promptly stomped off toward our hut. I fell in behind, trying to stifle a snicker that was bittersweet. Indeed, how much more shit could be piled on?

By morning's light, we were presented before the men of Major Todd. They were light infantry and they could be heard making comments about the unnecessary, burdensome addition of rangers. We were impassive to these comments and made an appearance as to not hear their words. Major Todd apprised us of the situation and of our duties, which he seemed to minimize in any way he knew how. The ladies who had provided unending comforts to Hobbs' Company had come to see us off. They gathered together in a tight circle, attempting to comfort one another. Abigail held Hannick with one arm around his waist, he sitting on her hip. Her small, bulging belly that had begun to present itself the past few days stood out with greater distinction that morning. Her other hand gently scratched at Namoosh's ears. Namoosh had a most peculiar look of concern on her face and did not stand, as usually she did, with her tongue hanging casually – rather she watched on with a most distraught expression. As Timms gave out his orders, I looked at her and could hear her whimpering, which brought me much sadness. I finally allowed my eyes to wander up to Abigail, who was herself holding back tears. At the lieutenant's closure, we were allowed to huddle near a small fire that would be last of such comforts for awhile.

"Boys, you will enjoy a final merriment before we make for the west," Todd announced. "I have asked my beautiful wife to play a parting tune for you all. So, enjoy it well and praise her properly!"

In the past few days, he had paraded Catherine about the fort, more like a trophy than a companion. It tore at my soul, but I knew no way to approach her as he always held her within his gaze.

Catherine stepped forward with her fiddle in hand. She gave a shallow bow to us and then began playing. As so long ago, I was transfixed and seemed to float on each little sound that she produced. Absolute silence fell over the men as they, too, listened with great intensity. A few pipes were lit and hot cups of various beverages were passed amongst the small groupings of brothers. We each thought on our fates and knew that we would be challenged by a thousand dangers in the weeks and months to follow. By now, most had become acquainted with the fort that stood at the confluence of the Niagara River and Lake Ontario. Tales were spread of a great, monstrous castle that was impenetrable by any but God's own angels. And Catherine's song continued on. Finally, we were told to make our goodbyes, so we approached those that we would be long in seeing. I separated Patrick and Abigail for only a moment, as I knew their parting time was in greater need. I held Abigail tightly and asked her to watch over Namoosh.

"You come back to me, brother. All of you, not just some damn shadow of the fine young man I see now before me. I love you, Solomon," Abigail choked out through her tears.

I knew that I would be unable to reply to her without crying myself, so I drew her closer and squeezed the back of her neck with my hand. I was then obliged to give an embrace to the other ladies, and then I separated myself from the tearful group. In the earlier hours, before day had broken, I had gone off by myself and plucked my hair back to a proper scalp-lock. I had braided the long, remaining hairs and had affixed a fine red shock of deer hair to my crown. I had, also, painted my face in the traditional way of a warrior, with reds, blacks, yellows, and whites. Timms said that I looked like a proper demon in my attire. This was my appearance as I walked to the edge of the company and as near to Catherine as I dared. I carefully watched Major Todd as he was cajoled by several officers who would be remaining at Fort William Henry. He was quite busy with this affair and thus did not see Catherine walk near to me and press a small bundle into my hand and lean in to say, "Be watchful, Solomon. Be watchful and return soon – I will be waiting."

She continued on her way after that moment at my side that could have been mistaken for nothing more than a thoughtful pause. I shoved the bundle into the open place in my shirt and felt it settle down inside, near my sash. I did not have the courage to watch her retreat. I simply continued to my place, now with even more to think upon in this early hour. Lieutenant Timms was reviewing his route map, and I went to him. I looked over the map with him as he explained where I was to go and what to be cautious of on the trail. Lastly, without appearing to deviate from his explanations, he asked me what I thought Catherine had given me. I looked at him with surprise and he brought his face from the map with a grin.

"Come now, boy, don't you know that your eyes give away too much? It will be our secret," Timms assured. "Now, get down the path. We'll be right behind you."

With this, I ran. I made a quick scan of the wooded edge and then plunged into the forest. My glance back caught Major Todd giving a terse kiss and a pat on the head of Catherine, which sent my blood ablaze. I then looked to the soldiers as they were ordered into their lines and the rangers out front, ambling as they best saw fit.

XX.

Our pace was faster than I supposed it would be, and we traversed the paths to Schenectady without incident.

In Schenectady, we met with the major force that had been drawn together to oppose the French at Niagara. General Prideaux was the commanding officers among our lines. He had gathered many officers and soldiers, including one of whom I stood in awe. Sir William Johnson had been a name that I had heard a thousand times in the preceding years. He had begun as a trader and had risen to become held in great esteem by both English and Indians alike. Sir William had brought a great force of the Iroquois Nation. He had been assured by them that it was their utmost desire that the French be removed from the land of the Seneca, a member of their great confederacy. It was good to be in the company of so many other Indian warriors, and as preparations were laid, I spent a great deal of time conferring with them. Some said that they had been in the fort at Niagara, and they explained it in great detail to me. Niagara was a massive, stone fortress with many cannon. It was situated on a slightly elevated point of land that defended the confluence of the Niagara River and Lake Ontario. It held a small port with a few ships that kept it readily supplied from other French holdings to the north.

These warriors stated that the French man, Pouchot, believed that there would be little danger from the English from the east. He had become so confident in the words given him by the Iroquois that he had relieved some of his men to march south. His goal was to regain the lands in the Ohio Country that had been lost in earlier campaigns. The Iroquois had assured Pouchot that they thought of the French as allies. This they once had indeed been – but now the alliance was but a betrayal, a ruse the Iroquois had undertaken because the French had betrayed them. This brought confidence to me and the others.

On the morning that we left to Schenectady to begin further west, we filled the many bateau and whale boats that had been wrought for this push. Time was needed for the men to adjust to this very different platform. We, accustomed to the presence of solid ground underfoot, needed practice in these crafts that were at the mercy of the rolling tide. Each boat held about sixteen men. We supposed that, with the aid of the Iroquois, we would pass through their lands unscathed. But early on we realized that this was not to be assured. One morning, some of the men who were charged with steering and caring for the boats put ashore without their guns. Immediately musket fire erupted from the forest and soon seven of them were dead and one carried away. The remaining boatmen were deeply chastised to never go anywhere without their firelocks, a lesson already deeply instilled in us woodsmen. The Iroquois were deeply insulted that this ambush could occur in their homeland, and they became enraged at the prospect of enemy warriors lurking in the area. Sir William encouraged them to remain true to the goal of attacking Fort Niagara, and his words were held in great solemnity by the warriors. He continued to send his loyal scouts to take false returns to the French officers and General Pouchot, which greatly aided our passage.

Great evidence of this area's volatility was present in every stop we made. Many small forts had been constructed. Sometimes these were little more than strong houses made of stone and equipped with loopholes in the walls to aid in repelling attackers. This was an area of perpetual warfare, and we became acquainted with the inhabitants and their well wishes for our campaign, they hoping that our endeavor would bring a greater peace to them. We frequently saw enemy scouts trying to access our strength and numbers. It was later discovered that the information they gleaned was always poor and did nothing to prepare Fort Niagara for our arrival.

By the end of June we had gained Fort Oswego at the far eastern end of Lake Ontario. This fort had just recently been recaptured from the French, who had taken possession of it in a past season. At Oswego the officers convened and made their selections as to which men would continue on and which men would stay to garrison the fort. A decision was made to send the very best two thousand men and one hundred officers to attack Niagara. Hobbs' Company was to continue with Major Todd's light infantry for the battle. We were placed in boats on the first of July. Again, about sixteen men to each boat was the order of the day. We, with the light infantry and grenadiers, were sent to watch the furthest regions of our flotilla's forward and rear. The grenadiers were hellish fellows. Most were giants of men made to appear even greater by tall, imposing hats. Each grenadier seemed the very image of Goliath. They wore the bright red regimental coats of regulars, but also carried metal bombs called grenades that were fixed with short fuses. In the crossed belts that lay over their coats they carried a short brass fixture that held a match kept ever-smoldering when in battle. They used this brass match to light the grenades. When an attack began, they could always be seen in the thickest of the fight, battling like crazed men.

The first day we traveled about thirty miles to a large bay that we set in to for shelter. The soldiers were becoming increasingly anxious as we neared our destination. This being the first night away from heavy walls and into the wilderness, the stories and tales flourished among them. The men seemed to dislike the presences of the six hundred Iroquois warriors, questioning the Indians' intentions and loyalties. Faith in these foreign men, who seemed so different from the soldiers, was not easily come by even in these urgent times. In contrast, the move away from the British fort seemed to place the Indian warriors at greater ease, we being well-placed in the shelter of our natural surroundings.

Our second day saw us another thirty-five miles closer to our destination. The following morning was greeted by furious winds that so defied us that we were made to stay in that place an additional day, bringing more time to reflect on what might befall us. I became enthralled by the excitement that surged through both red and white men. They were made to suppose themselves the most invincible of siege men. It is an illusion I have encountered many times since. It is a confidence that men must exude to assure their own souls of their capability. I have thought deeply on this, and I now reckon that it must be done or else no man would willingly face the nightmares of the storms of lead and iron that are dealt out in war.

The day after our stalled journey, we made twenty miles. The officers explained that this would be our last stopping point before coming ashore near Fort Niagara. Men reserved these moments to either pray or get drunk on smuggled spirits, each seeing fit to make his own final moments of peace before the siege would open. Hobbs' Company was made to camp with Todd's light infantry, but as always we managed to make our own area a bit apart from the rest. In these final hours before we would fall into our attack, the veterans such as Timms and Crum saw to conveying all useful information contained within their experiences to better prepare us. Lieutenant Timms encouraged us to fight bravely but to not throw our lives away on an ignorant task, while Crum drove into our minds to fight hard and mercilessly, as our enemy would have no mercy upon us. Timms went on to explain what had happened at Fort William Henry a few years earlier. The French had set to siege the fort and had been very successful. At the end, the British were unable to hold the fort and were forced to surrender. The French officers had given very easy terms of capitulation, but upon exiting the fort, the soldiers were attacked by Indians who were enraged that they had no plunder or scalps.

"I saw, several times, as warriors led several of our men away from our column to butcher them in the woods," Timms recounted through clenched teeth. "The cowards never made attempts at those of us who would stand together and not permit their savagery, but any who strayed were killed. They knew no mercy to the weak or injured; their thoughts were given over completely to greed and bloodlust. Those were scenes from hell, but we were so defeated and discouraged that the most heroic deed we could do was to preserve ourselves and the few closest to us. I will not forget that day, and God willing I will have a chance to repay it."

Timms' vehemence burned through his words. He rubbed a weathered hand over his face as if to brush away the memories, and then he stared at us with those piercing eyes.

"Be careful, boys," he said. "Fight hard, as Patrick has said. This will not be like the skirmishes in the forest, where it ends quickly; this business will take awhile, so fight well and sell your lives dearly."

We were not permitted to have a fire, but Timms lit a single candle that we gathered around on this final night. We continued our council until an emissary of General Prideaux arrived with two red sashes and a note from the general. It stated that one sash was to be worn by Timms. He was to appoint a sergeant who would receive the other. There, in the small light, Timms called forward Patrick, around whose waist he wrapped the second sash.

"Fight well, lads. Bring honor to Captain Hobbs' memory and to yourselves. Sergeant Crum, you know well to lead these men if I should fall," Lieutenant Timms explained in those late hours.

Crum's elevation was protested by no one, each man seeing him as the natural leader in Timms' absence. Our conversations slowly shifted from our duties to life after the upcoming battle. I reserved these moments to reopen the bundle that Catherine had given me. My thumb slid over her written words, and I pressed the small cloth scarf, which had also been contained in the package, to my nose. The scarf bore several neatly stitched flowers, as well as Catherine's initials.

Soon the time drew near when we would attempt a few hours of rest, with some men left to keep watch. I rolled up Catherine's scarf and tied it to my wrist so that it would be near at all times. I refolded her note and placed it in my pouch and then said my evening prayer. I supposed that all could be lost in the next few days, but I also clung to the hope that I would return and see her again.

Images of her face drifted through my mind as I fell into a brief and fitful sleep.

XXI.

The next afternoon we came to within four miles of Fort Niagara. We spent the remainder of the day dragging the small boats ashore. At dusk I was sent with several Iroquois and light infantrymen to reconnoiter the fort's defenses. As we drew near, we discovered several French men who were hunting pigeons. The Iroquois and I, somewhat ahead of the regular soldiers, fired upon them – and they surged at us immediately, meaning to repel what they believed to be nothing more than an Indian raiding party. As they pursued us, we fell behind the light infantry, who gave them a proper volley, heralding the start of the siege. The French made a hasty retreat, leaving one dead man behind. An Iroquois warrior went to him and scalped the dead soldier and removed his coat.

That night, the warrior and his brethren danced about in a furious manner and encouraged me to join them. Stripped to little more than breechcloths and leggings, we raised our muskets and tomahawks in victorious rage and brought ourselves to a great lather. The captured French regimental coat was blue with white facings. It seemed to make its own dance as it swirled about its new owner, the tails spinning out and down with each leaping step the frenzied warrior took. To the other officers' dismay, Sir William Johnson joined us in this dance and showed his true spirit. Like us, he danced with a tomahawk in hand and moved like he had been taught by his Mohawk brothers. As we danced in our circle, our figures lit by a small fire, one warrior would detach himself from the whole and rush a stout pole that had been erected near the fire.

In a show of expert fighting skill, he would spin, twirl or duck near the pole, as it represented the enemy. Finally, in the most furious moment of the dance, he would strike with incredible force at the pole, which would emit a thunderous cracking sound. We each took our turn, showing our fellows our abilities. In an image of respect, William Johnson was permitted to go last. His feet fell lightly on the crushed earth surrounding the pole. His eyes rolled in his head and his face snapped from side to side seeking out the foe. The hard thumping of the drum had him dancing with quick steps, and in the final beat he leapt from the ground, bringing his waist to the height of most men's heads. He swung the tomahawk backwards in a hard, fluid motion and buried the blade of the tomahawk deep into the "head" of the pole. This elicited tremendous screams and howls from we who surrounded him, and we all rushed in to meet together in a mighty knot of brotherhood.

I returned to my company fully exhausted and covered in sweat. I was eyed by the new men with suspicion, they being fully unaware of my peoples' customs. I learned later that our dance and drum had struck fear into both British and French hearts that night. Timms and Crum came to me with smiles and hopes that the rest of our campaign would be so one-sided as the attack on the hunting party. I crashed to my blankets and stared at the stars above. I hoped that what we were engaged in would be looked upon as just in the eyes of the Lord and that He would grant us victory.

The next morning, the grenadiers, assisted by rangers and light infantry, were sent to attack a schooner that lay near the fort. The short battle was quickly decided by the fort's great guns. They pounded hard at the whale boats and drove them away from the ship. The cannons' roar was deafening even from afar, and I could not imagine being next to the things when they were touched off. The cannon balls rained down on the small boats, smashing one to pieces and lifting the boatmen and soldiers high into the air before dropping them all over the water like so many leaves blown in the wind. The schooner's men shot at the stranded English and, as Crum had predicted, showed no mercy when confronted by their desperate pleas. Later, the same schooner, named *Iroquoise*, was sent to attack us at the stream where we had come ashore. Its attempts to disrupt our activity were weak, and the boatmen in our company jeered their efforts while the *Iroquoise* guns pounded at our camp with their small artillery pieces. At one point, the schooner drew so near that the fearless grenadiers rushed to the shoreline and attempted to fire their grenades into the ship. One grenade exploded just as it arched down towards the schooner's gunwales, knocking three or four men away from the rail. The explosion caused huge splinters to spray in all directions, including toward those standing near the rail. One man gave out a scream – a long, thin shard jutted from his impaled leg. This was deterrence enough, and the cowardly ship commander drew his *Iroquoise* away from the counterattack. The slow tack of the ship away from our camp brought cheers from our men, and some even sought to chase the fleeing ship with musket balls that splashed the water around it and occasionally thumped into its transom.

We continued to scout the area as the remainder of the soldiers were set hard at constructing camp, unloading boats, and dragging the heavy cannons toward a trench that had been opened the preceding night at the edge of the fort's clearing. General Prideaux sent one of his officers to seek parlay with the French garrison. The officer carried a white flag as he walked into the clearing. He was stopped outside the fort gate and blindfolded. A few hours later, he returned and stated that, while he was treated well inside the fort by General Pouchot, he was given a statement that the French would not surrender. That night as the trench was continued, Sir William Johnson sent several of his Iroquois to scout very near the fort. Timms sent me with them. I skulked through a cemetery with a clutch of Iroquois. We were viewing the men standing on the wall when we heard a commotion a short distance away. We bent close to ground, passing from stone to stone, and soon saw the makers of the noise. Pouchot had sent out his own scouts, and they had in turn run into our fellows in the graveyard. Each side, being startled by the meeting, began firing blind shots at the other. We fell back and took shelter as we watched one Huron, who had outdistanced his fellows, go running back to join his party. They, being still rattled by the appearance of our party, shot their own man as he returned. We had by now become well acquainted with this sort of mistaken killing, and as we regained friendly territory, we vowed that we would be more careful in our own aim if ever we were presented with a like situation.

Many more mistakes occurred in the following days. As the sun's light revealed the newly constructed yards of British trench to the French defenders, the fort's guns exploited a fatal miscalculation. The trench had been dug at the wrong angle, allowing the French to fire directly into the ditch and upon the men working. Two were killed before they could extract themselves and throw up some barriers to stop Niagara's guns from destroying all that had been done. As the English officers conferred about the error, the defenders threw another surprise our way. Pouchot had sent men to gather pickets outside of the fort so that he could construct embrasures, bundles of sticks meant to absorb enemy fire. The small party of soldiers came very near to our trench and saw that it was empty. They, being encouraged by no opposition, attempted to rush into the trench in hopes of reaching us and sweeping away their attackers. Shouts were heard all through our camp as soldiers snatched their muskets from the stacks and rushed to fight those who had gained the trench. The men acted without orders, and ragged fire spread all along the open ground. Both British and French officers were screaming at their men to fall into orderly arrangements. The French, to cover the retreat of their men, began firing their great cannons at the British soldiers standing in the open. The huge balls flew in our direction, splintering and even cutting down the trees in their path. I saw one British soldier standing at the top of the trench plunging his bayonet into several French soldiers who were attempting to gain his height. As he jabbed the final time, he turned to run back toward camp and was struck by a cannon ball that completely removed his head. A fine red mist floated up from his body, which continued to stand for a moment before limply falling backwards into the trench. The sight of this made most of the other soldiers run back to our lines, and the whole affair of the sally was over by the time the sun reached its place high overhead.

General Prideaux, incensed by the French gall in attacking his trench, sent forward the smallest of his artillery the next day. The small guns were called cohorns. They were used to lob large grenades, about the size of a man's fist, into the fort. The distant sound of their explosion could be heard in our camp. Much discussion was made as to what effect the cohorns were having on the garrison. The French seemed to answer the bombs with a more furious cannon fire. The British gunners attempted to drop their bombs on the men manning the fort guns but were very inaccurate with their fire and did nothing to disrupt the cannons. This game was kept up through the day and into the early dusk until the two sides could no longer see each other or where they were firing. When full darkness had fallen over all, the trenchers restarted their work, digging at a furious pace. Likewise, we were worked beyond exhaustion as Major Todd set us rangers to the most dangerous of tasks, he having little regard for our safety. It was evident that he was attempting to rid himself of our presence, and he seemed dismayed each early morning when we returned uninjured from our nocturnal missions.

The morning after the daylong artillery exchange, upon questioning a fellow soldier I discovered that the day was the 12th of July. It was the time of the day when men could no longer dig at the sap and just before the cannon fire could be aimed. I enjoyed the moments of quiet to watch birds flitting along the branches and small animals scampering about. The first shots from the fort or trench would always drive them off, but I was amazed to see their return each morning, they perhaps hoping this whole mess had come to an end. Lieutenant Timms, Sergeant Crum, Fehn, and I were heating a small kettle of water to be used for making chocolate. As we did this, we watched the heavy cannons being dragged into the trench. Both British and French had awaited their arrival and their being brought into play. As the huge iron beasts were lowered into the trench, a whistling shot announced the fire from that damned old schooner *Iroquoise.* Several men were made to jump in to the trench after the cannons. One gun was dropped on a poor fellow, who was speedily relieved by his fellows as they lifted the massive thing off of him. The *Iroquoise* harassed us with fire for a short while longer and, after having affected us little, continued sailing on and out of sight, eastward across the lake. The cannons were laid out throughout the trench and were closely watched by their gunners, who cursed soldiers who, running along, would inadvertently kick rocks and soil into the barrels. The gunners finally dug into their boxes and found huge round plugs that they jammed into the mouths of the cannons to prevent their corruption.

At dusk we were preparing to go on our evening scout. The few engineers who had accompanied this campaign came walking along the lines of soldiers. Muffled insults rippled along the lines, as the soldiers had become quite irritated by the apparent incompetence of the engineers, who had enabled the bloody French incursion a few days ago. I stood to watch them pass into the trench while I dug at the ashy crust around the lock on my musket with my knife tip. Most of the French cannons had slowed their fire as night came, and so silence had been gained again. Men went about their various tasks that dealt with both their duties and personal needs. Suddenly, a blast sounded from the fort and a screaming cannon ball rushed across the open ground and into the edge of the sap. When the ringing in our ears had stopped, we could hear shouts erupting from the trench, and several men went running toward the calls for aid. A short while later, Chief Engineer Williams was carried out of the trench on blanket that was held by six men. They rushed by our camp and I saw Williams pressing a large cloth to his face. As they continued on, I saw Williams' arms slump, limply, off the blanket edge. Porter, who had been in the sap when the cannon ball hit, came running back to us and excitedly reported what had occurred. He stated that Williams was laying out the location for the battery to be constructed for the British cannons when the French fired their own cannon. The ball had plowed through the edge of the trench and hit Williams in the face, knocking him across the trench and nearly burying him in the disrupted earth.

"Thought for sure the bastard was dead, but then he started moaning and thrashing about, so we started digging him out and those other men came along and carried him up out of there!" Porter said with excited flourish.

We continued to watch as Williams' successor was sent back into the trench to continue his superior's work. And then we were sent out, once again, into the darkness. Throughout the night we saw men sneaking from the fort, heading south. As hard as we worked, we were unable to stop all of them, and it was well known that they would be going in search of relief forces. This knowledge weighed heavily on us all, as none knew of the location or strength of the men who might return to assist the fort's defenders.

Morning's light brought another disappointment. The battery that had been laid out by Williams and completed in the night hours was facing the wrong direction. This brought more curses upon the engineers. Prideaux had grown exceedingly irritated by these continued mishaps. Lieutenant Timms, returning from a meeting with the officers, stated that it had been estimated we had received about 6,000 shots from the fort's cannons. That seemed like a huge number, and it did not seem as if the fort could contain much more shot; but each day the French continued their heavy fire. Our spirits began to sink, and murmurs became common as to the possibility that we might fail in our endeavor. More and more men became concerned with what might appear from the south to relieve the fort. To add to the mounting concern, all of our Iroquois allies were called to a meeting inside the fort with General Pouchot. A war captain amongst the Mohawk bid me to accompany the small party of Iroquois emissaries, and asked only that I curtail my sharp tongue as there would be very sensitive matters discussed within the fort. I was told by another of my Mohican brothers that this was a great honor to be asked to this council, so I reluctantly gave over my musket to Sergeant Crum and joined the council as we adorned ourselves in the most ornate clothing and paint as could be gained in this far-removed place.

General Pouchot was seated on a beautifully gilded chair that seemed to sparkle. It easily caught our eyes as we walked through the strong Gate of Six Nations that was the entrance to Fort Niagara. The name bestowed on the gate had been given in honor to those upon whose territory this beastly structure had been wrought, and who now helped in its besiegement. It was clear that, before our arrival, the general had gone to great extent to try to clean up the destruction that had been played on his fort. The most healthy and uninjured fellows were drawn into lines to give the impression of strong resolve, but Pouchot had not been able to fully conceal all that had occurred here. My fellow war leaders and I proudly strolled up the cobblestone roadway that led to the main grounds of the fort. Leading us was one extremely tall and regal-looking Seneca sachem who wore upon his head the crown of his people. An ornate headdress of eagle and turkey feathers rose high above his face, with several curly turkey feathers trailing down to his shoulders. The true mark of his significance, though, were the deer antlers that protruded from each side of his head as they had once done on that of their original owner. Several other sachems also wore these headdresses, denoting them as the true leaders of our council. The differences in each adornment denoted their respective tribes. I, having no significance in the overall leadership – simply being honored by fellow warriors as having been exemplary in this particular engagement – had nothing to denote any importance except for a fine matchcoat that had been gifted to me just prior to our departure for the fort. The Mohawk leader who had seen fit to invite me to this council had given me a large swath of red wool that was bordered around its entire edge by a wide, gold silk ribbon. I understood the significance of this, as a matching one had been given, a long time ago, to another Mohican man by a Mohawk leader when they had come to understand a good peace between those two tribes. I proudly draped my new matchcoat over my shoulder and around my waist, tucking it in lightly so as to not obscure too much of the gold ribbon that bordered it; I felt as important as any along on this errand because I was representing Stockbridge and its people.

Mostly we looked straight toward where we were going in the parade grounds, but as they could our eyes darted here and there, noting the damage to this or that structure. Also, not being deaf, I could hear the screams of soldiers who had been the victims of our shelling as were now victims of their own surgeons; the sound was horrifying, and it was only stifled when thick oaken doors were slammed shut before our prying eyes.

XXII.

General Pouchot rose to meet us and gave us a great bow, casting the tails of his coat far out behind him and rolling his three-cornered hat in a manner well-practiced by men in his realm. With his hand, he motioned for us to sit. We did so, forming a half-circle that was completed by his half-circle of officers. A large pipe was lit by a Mohawk and then began making its way around our circle. The pipe was of the style which had been borrowed from far western tribes; it was made of two pieces – a stone bowl, coupled with a wooden stem that was half the length of my bow. The bowl was made of a dull red stone that many of our people consider to be the remnants of the blood of our elders – they who died in the Great Flood. The stem was ornately decorated with feathers and quillwork. The whole effect of this pipe and the pomp established by the French gave the scene a most lofty air. No words were exchanged as each man kept to the sacredness of this ceremony. Words did not pass, but looks certainly did as each man sought out his opposite across the circle and met his eyes with probing intensity. When the pipe had been passed fully about our circle, General Pouchot rose from his chair and addressed us with utmost respect; indeed, more respect than we had ever received from the English officers with whom we served. The words were in French, and the Mohawk leader who sat to my right translated for me. Gifts were offered, gifts of blankets, kettles, silver, knives, and many of the other trinkets that white men use to persuade Indians at council. These were accepted with thanks, and at Pouchot's conclusion each among our party arose, one by one, and gave his testimony as to whether or not we should continue this fight between our two sides.

To General Pouchot's credit, he did not attempt to draw us to his side; he simply sought to convince us to walk away from this squabble which he stated was between white men and which was not our concern. Many took this as an offense, particularly the Seneca, who stated that this was their land and that the fort was constructed beyond the permission they had granted for the establishment of a simple trading post. The general gave this to be true, but explained that he had only allowed it out of the great love that he felt for his Iroquois brothers and due to his sincere hopes to aid in their defense and security. This softened the hearts of the many, and in the end many wampum belts of peace were passed between the opposing councilors. An agreement was made that the Iroquois would draw themselves away from the fight; I was deeply upset by this conclusion. The major sachems had spoken – and, my anger being evident, the Mohawk leader leaned over to rationalize the decision to me. He explained that, because the British trenches had drawn so near the fort, it was to the Iroquois' benefit to be relieved of their duty. Otherwise, they would only be cannon fodder if left between these two forces that would begin to fight furiously in the next few days. His words eased me, in sorts, but I still found it hard to believe they could not find anything more important to do than abandon the fight. I questioned him; to this he responded by slapping me hard on the shoulder and giving me his broad smile.

"Do not worry, Solomon," he said. "We'll not be far off!"

I looked deeply into his face and realized the meaning of his words.

"Is there any other nation who wishes to speak in regard to what has been said?" asked a translator among the French councilors.

I thought on these words for only half a second, and then found myself standing. The Mohawk grabbed at my arm and held me in a stoop.

"Please!" he begged. "Say nothing that will disrupt this treaty."

"What I have to say is for my people," was all that I could assure him.

I felt all faces turn my way as I drew myself to my full height amidst a sea of urgent whispers – mostly leaders trying to ascertain my identity. I stood silently for a long moment until the whispering subsided. A final glance toward the Mohawk at my side let me know that he might have been regretting bringing me along.

"I am Solomon of the Stockbridge Indians," I began.

This cleared up my identity to some and imparted yet others with even more confused looks.

"For many years we have stood by our English Brothers," I continued. Now I had gained the intense stare of one French-allied warrior, whom I supposed by his appearance and hateful countenance was an Abenaki. I met his stare and proceeded. "When first they came to this place, we were great and they were small. Now, they have become great and we are small – but we still hold true to our oaths. I say to you, my brothers to the west, that I shall fight my English brothers' enemy. I will take hold of his heel so that he cannot run so easily as if I were not there. Ever we have considered the English as a great tree, whose shade underneath which we gather for protection. And I tell you this, my brothers and my enemies, that if this great tree shall fall, then we shall fall with it!"

My words brought silence and stillness from all save the Abenaki, who had to be caught by several French soldiers as he made a quick approach toward me. He brought from behind his back a large and ancient wooden war club which he no doubt had produced in the hopes of ending my life. I did not flinch as he came within a pace of striking me down and was then stopped by the soldiers; rather, I stood with a set face and watched as he was harshly dragged away. I, too, was dragged from my feet – dragged back to my blanket by several elders, out of fear that I might jeopardize the peace that had been made. I had not been bent on hatred, but simply upon stating what occupied my mind, knowing as I did that I would not join the Iroquois in some safe place a few miles away – that, rather, I would maintain my place at the sides of my white brothers whom I had come to love as my own kin.

Final, hasty words were exchanged between the two sides, and then our party made a quick departure from the fort.

Word of what had been decided spread like fire among the British troops, and they cast their most horrible curses towards the Iroquois warriors as the Indians gathered together their few things and began a slow progression south. I rejoined my company, and all looked upon me to ascertain my own decision.

"Will you go?" Timms asked as he sat down at my side.

I did not meet his face, but looked instead on the heavy walls of the fort that I supposed I would break myself against in the next few days. With a deep sigh, I answered.

"Not if all hell's demons were unleashed from over those ramparts," I gave him.

My fellows encircled me, then, and treated me with the finest words that those hard men could muster. I knew that I had made the proper decision, whatever fate would play.

XXIII.

The siege continued. Nights achieved a taxing sameness as we pressed on in our duties. Our nocturnal scouts became increasingly perilous because the trench had drawn so near the fort that little space was left for us to range. The morning after the Iroquois had left the British camp, those that still remained in the fort abandoned the French; they who had originally supported our enemy now did like their brethren and abandoned their European ties. As they left Niagara, they shot the fort's remaining livestock and presented it to the British troops to help sooth any feelings of ill will. From our encampment they continued south to join with their fellows at a place called La Belle Famille, nearly a mile south of Fort Niagara. The British dined on the fresh meat and briefly forgot their anger.

The sappers took on a furiously pitched pace, as they supposed that ever foot they gained brought them closer to the fort walls – but, more importantly, closer to home. As our proximity to the fort drew nearer, more creative and hellish means of killing men were employed. Men the likes of Thomas Fehn were placed in our trench and, with their deadly rifles, made short the lives of French soldiers who stood on the walls. Cannon shot began to dwindle, and gunners began excavating spent French cannon balls that they dusted off, quickly inspected, and then sent back to their original owners; British iron was fired on Brits, and French iron upon French. Even when not made to work from the trench, Thomas Fehn and a clutch of his own like dealt a horrible hand to any of the enemy who attempted to peek over the walls. The three would slowly scan the walls, two watching for any other sharpshooters, while the third leveled and fired. This kept on until they either saw no targets or the scarcity of light no longer permitted their hunt.

Fehn returned to our camp one early morning, and I studied him closely as he cleaned his rifle. Age had crept up on him, and he no longer held the soft appearance of a simple squirrel hunter. He paused from his cleaning and let his weapon lay across his knees as he looked sideways into the trench and toward the distant wall. He turned back and caught me viewing him as he sat lost in his thoughts.

"Solomon, does God punish us if we kill men in battle?" he asked. His words seemed like those of a child.

"The Bible says not," I gave outwardly, nonetheless unsure on the inside, chided by the nagging of a deeper voice.

"Lieutenant Timms said that I was supposed to shoot those men if they looked at the trench, and that's what we did," Fehn said. "You know, they were shooting at us, too? They just can't shoot like we can and we always get them. But we're supposed to do that, right?"

Fehn's questions persisted, and I had no answer. I could barely justify my own actions, my own sins – and he was my age, or thereabout. I was not a good friend that day and regret that I had nothing loftier to give him. Given the many years that have passed since then, I suppose now that I could tell him more to ease his mind; but I also suppose my answer might still be just as lacking in true wisdom. Truly, this matter of righteous bloodshed will remain a mystery until we arrive at the day when we can ask the Almighty – or discover His views through His wrath. Alas, my final answer to Fehn on that long-ago day was that he should just do whatever Timms told him to do and try not to get shot; I could think of nothing else, and was truly sorry for it. Thomas returned to his cleaning, and I crept away when the tension of the moment had eased. Questions such as these have haunted me since, and never did I relish their arrival.

On July 17th, the morning was as foggy as an early spring day in Stockbridge. The joy of this was the lack of fire from either side, but in it lay terror, as well. Men's minds seem to wander at such moments, and we supposed in the confusion of the thick air that we could be surrounded or that the fort's defenders would devise some other evil plan to carry out in the comfort of this thick shroud. None of these came to fruition, but as soon as the fog lifted, the first solid cannon shot was fired at the fort from the British lines. Across the river from where we had been digging our trench, a secret battery had been placed to host several of our large cannon. To the accompaniment of many cheers from our lines came the echoing sound of a cannon ball crashing into one of the chimneys of the fort's castle. A large plume of dust shot skyward as the hard ball disintegrated stone and mortar. The cracking sound rolled across our troops and made them cheer ever louder. Some soldiers whirled their fellows in circles with linked arms; this was the moment whose arrival both sides had been awaiting. The significance of this event cannot be overstated. When concerted, solid shot is brought into play against a fortification, no place can stand long. In the passing years, I have seen the devastation that it brings, and the thunder that enthralled me as a youth now dredges up horrible memories.

Not long after the first solid shots were fired on Fort Niagara, the *Iroquoise* reappeared on the horizon. I watched as the French, no doubt hoping for relief, hastily sent a canoe out to receive word from the ship. The men at the battery across the river, which had been named Montreal Point, appreciated this new target and fired a shot at the canoe which was delivered with such accuracy as to take the paddle out of the boatman's hands. It was a distant sight, but we watched as the little thing was clearly flung from the man's hands and he was forced to cower, bent over himself, in the tiny craft. British soldiers took this as a good omen, and the incident drove the morale to new heights. But their enthusiasm was not to last long, as soon the sun fell below the edge of the world.

That night, two high men died in their pursuit of victory. The first death was that of Colonel Johnston who, upon the discovery a few days earlier of the engineers' great deficiency, had taken to overseeing the construction of the trenches, greatly improving their development. His death came at the hands of a musket ball through the lung, delivered as he was surveying the head of the dig. As I have stated, the proximity that had been attained presented men on each side as easy targets to those with well- trained fire. So was the fate of Colonel Johnston, deeply beloved by his fellow soldiers. His service was well remembered. A short hour later, the evening's tragedy deepened tenfold. General Prideaux, our commanding officer, was attempting to establish order in the trench and continue its progression when he errantly stepped in front of an active mortar. He was struck by a round and died instantly. The effect of his death was nearly disastrous, as officers convened and attempted to ascertain General Prideaux's rightful replacement. Sir William Johnson was the next in line because of his rank and title, but his attempts at taking command were contested by those who believed that a "proper" regular officer should take the lead. Sir William prevailed, though, and soon explained that he would stay true to the orders previously established by the late General Prideaux.

Now that the big guns had been established in their place, the fort could not long hold out. It seemed it would be but a few days until the fort and its defenders were brought to their knees. But before it was to fall, our lines were overcome by news of a horrible discovery: French reinforcements had begun to draw near. Word was received from a courier that a large mass of irregular French troops were drawing close to La Belle Famille. Immediately, we were sent with the grenadiers and Major Todd's light infantry to attempt to intercept these troops. As we were drawing into the woods to prepare for the skirmish, the light infantry split from us and began placing logs to create a makeshift emplacement. The Iroquois, who had abandoned us a few days earlier, stood to our left and appeared to watch on in great interest. Soon the enemy appeared through the trees; they fired en masse at the first opportunity. Firing all the while, they drew nearer and nearer; the fighting became quite hellish, and in the very midst of the very worst fighting were the fearless grenadiers. They rushed from their cover and ran so near the French that they could fire their muskets and lob their grenades with startling accuracy. A few of them were cut down by the ragged volleys that the French attempted, but soon the enemies were breaking rank and running. Behind us, we could hear the futile attempts that Fort Niagara was taking to weaken our position and assist its reinforcements. The French fired several of their cannons, but to no effect because of the great range. The Iroquois, seeing that the tide had turned against the French, began firing into the French troops' flank and successfully aided us in breaking their approach. The Iroquois gave great chase after the fleeing enemy and were covered in gore and scalps by the time that they returned to our camp.

The fort surrendered, having little left in the way of ammunition and supplies – and much in the way of broken spirits – and with no hope of relief. In hopes of not recreating the terrible acts that had been committed against our troops at Fort William Henry, Sir William Johnson used every bit of his persuasion to keep his Indian allies in check. Despite his greatest efforts, he was unable to completely stop them from pillaging those who had surrendered; but, all things considered, he did a much finer job than another might have done.

All were relieved to be finished with the fighting. I saw it on the faces of Iroquois warriors and British and French soldiers alike. The soldiers and officers who had been captured would be sent back east; the soldiers would be jailed, the officers ransomed. The grenadiers, along with many of the regular troops who had been dispatched to siege this fort, would be left to garrison their new prize. Sir William Johnson gathered together his officers to confer with them about a party to be sent to escort of the prisoners. All had hoped on having time to recuperate from the long siege, but our luck did not see to it. Major Todd was named as the primary officer who would escort the prisoners, and we would be sent to assist him. Sir William did not want to waste any time in removing the prisoners, in the case that the French should send fresh troops from the North. He would be busy in refortifying Niagara and did not want to be bothered with the strenuous duty of jailing so many captives. Neither did he want to face the threat of a revolt in the instance that they might see an opportunity to hatch one.

XXIV.

In stark contrast to the relatively dignified way in which the white prisoners were handled, the Indian prisoners were handed over to the Iroquois for them to do with as they saw fit. Sir William had little recourse, given that he did not have the means or men to hold them. As we lined up the French soldiers for their long march, the Iroquois were loading their prisoners with mounds of plunder, as much as could be carried. They led them away while giving out great whoops of victory and spewing abusive language upon their enemies. We walked our prisoners to the whale boats and secured them in such a way that they could do the greatest share of the rowing while we would stand guard. The wind blew hard against us, not being impeded by any strong land feature in the midst of the flat terrain. With great effort, we pushed from the shore and began the long journey home. Reaching open water, the boatmen deployed small sails, as the winds were now in our favor. It relieved the prisoners to know that at least they would not have to pull themselves for the entire voyage across the waters to their own prisons.

    The second night of our sail brought us ashore near some small hills. I stretched out the fatigue that had built in my arms in legs during the long days on the water. Squatting down near the shoreline, I took a small handful of gravel and let the small pebbles sift between my fingers. Looking over my shoulder, I saw Major Todd exiting his boat; I had to stifle my laughter as he nearly pitched into the water. Giving out a low sigh, I looked back to the pebbles falling between my fingers and then back up to the small hills. In the distance they appeared pleasant and softly rounded. I traced their progression to where we lay and saw that as they reached our shore they took on a sharp and accusatory appearance. I could not help but think of them as fingers pointing at us in a shameful way for the things we had done. The events of the past weeks swept over me, and I rose and began walking toward the pointed ridges to see to their accusations. They were steep and loosely built, and I scrambled to gain my grip as I hauled myself up the slopes. Upon finally reaching the top of the nearest ridge, I turned and watched as below the prisoners were led into a circle. Major Todd entered their center and began delivering a harsh speech of which, from my distance, I could only hear a bit. I shifted my gaze toward the beach and watched Hobbs' Company drag a boat ashore near our camp. Sergeant Crum came from the edge of the woods with a large stump that he used to prop up the edge of the boat. In this way they had constructed a small shelter that we could sleep under, thus keeping off the next day's dew or the evening's rain that seemed ever more imminent. I turned back towards the hills and stretched my arms toward them. Catherine's scarf peeked out from my sleeve and hung lazily there, fluttering ever so slightly. It was now covered in accumulated grime from the many days of fighting. I noticed that the filth did not stop with the cloth; rather, it crept up my arms, and I realized that I had not bathed in many days. I took note of the smell that clung to me: that of sweat and earth and dried blood. My arms outstretched, I held the setting sun between my hands and I gave out to the Creator a prayer imploring forgiveness. I likewise offered the same prayer to these hills that so hated me for reasons I had yet to understand.

The snapping of a twig brought me from my reverence, and I peered down the hillside to see a doe that moments before had been slowly picking her way through a ravine, but that was now frozen in her stance as she looked, with terror, over her shoulder. I followed her stare up the ravine and could see nothing that should have her in such a state of alarm. Just the same, I knelt and drew my firelock from where it hung at my side. Then they emerged. I now felt the doe's terror as I watched the members of a massive war party slipping stealthily from tree to tree. I tried to count their number, but it appeared that men were coming from behind every tree. The doe bolted, and the leader of the war party held up his hand to stop his men. Amazingly, she ran straight down the ravine toward our encampment. When she burst from the cover and out onto the beach, I saw her startle a soldier who was foraging for firewood.

"What the bloody hell?" he said as he stumbled backwards.

His fellows, seeing him start at a deer, began laughing at him, and some of them began shooting at the deer in the prospect of having fresh meat. I was about to alert them to the war party when I heard the crunch of leaves just a few paces behind me. I held still, not wanting to alert whoever might be behind me. Slowly the warrior crept into the edge of my vision. He had not seen me, but my throat was closed as if a tight hand had been clasped to it. As he looked away from me, scanning the woods, I gently brought my musket up to aim at the side of his head. I knew that when I brought the cock of my musket back that he would hear it, as he was only a pace away and I was only concealed by a single small shrub. But something had to be done. Glancing over my shoulder, I could see that the edge of the war party was moving again. Looking back to the warrior nearest me, I pushed the butt of the musket hard into my arm. In a fluid movement, I snapped back the cock; the warrior's head swung to face me. His eyes were as wide as can be imagined, and his jaw went slack as he looked down the barrel of my gun. In a brave but desperate move, he began to give a yell to alert his fellows, but I cut short his words when I pulled the trigger and sent a heavy ball crashing into his open mouth. I didn't wait to see him fall, as the war party acted immediately to my musket's report. Suddenly I was surrounded by balls snapping past my head from every direction. An arrow sang by my face and plunged deep into the tree at my side. I jumped to my feet and began running back down the slope.

"Ambush!" I screamed as I ran down the hillside.

The British soldiers looked on me in surprise and confusion as I kept up my screams of alert. The warriors were streaming over the hilltops as I reached Hobbs' Company and their boat. All around, soldiers were falling in mid-stride, cut down as they ran to their arms.

"Sweet mother of Jesus," Lieutenant Timms uttered as we watched the war party massacring the soldiers.

Sergeant Crum kicked aside the stump holding up the boat, and we rushed behind it as it provided the only cover available to us. We were caught between the water and the hellish attack. Lead was smacking the thin wood, and many balls were whistling through the places where the planks came together. The early night air was filled with the screams of warriors and dying men as we attempted to contrive a plan. We gave covering fire to our rangers who were not in camp at the time of the opening shots of the ambush.

"Crum, we have to get these men off this beach or we'll all be killed," Timms yelled. "Take Wheeler and Lockridge and move up to that point over there."

He pointed at a small hill that did not seem to be inundated with enemy warriors.

"We will give cover as you make your way there," Timms said. "Find a good place and then we'll come after. Go!"

I had just reloaded my musket and was looking over the keel of the overturned boat when I saw a mass of painted warriors rushing toward us.

"Timms! There!" I screamed.

We poured fire into them, and the remaining of their number broke off their rush and began circling toward the relative safety of some of the other boats. Fehn was on his hands and knees digging furiously under our own boat. Having made a small hole, he plunged his hand into it and dragged out a long box that he smashed open with the butt of his rifle. Inside, packed loosely in sawdust, were about a dozen grenades.

Lieutenant Timms smiled.

"Good work, boy," he said. "But we haven't one of those damn matches to light the bloody things."

"I have an idea. Solomon, get ready to fire," ordered Fehn.

I inched up to the side of the boat and prepared to shoot. I could feel Fehn pushing hard against my back as he leaned over me. He had scooped up three of the grenades, and as I fired at one of the warriors hiding behind a nearby boat, he held the wick against the lock of my musket. Instantly, I could hear the sizzling of the fuse. He held the other two grenades near the first, and soon they were all lit. In furious succession, he lobbed them at the boat nearest to us, which was concealing several men. The grenades bounced off the wooden hull and rolled over the edge just as they detonated. The explosions sent a spray of sand, rock, blood, and bone into the air and then showering down all around and on us. The boat had been obliterated, and we took this moment of shock on the enemy's part to start running toward the hill that Crum now held. As we rushed to the slope, we saw Lockridge lying face down in the sand. His musket was buried, muzzle down, and a huge dark spot was spreading over his back where a massive hole had been ripped through his shirt. As we passed by, Timms reached down and grabbed his musket. Crum and Wheeler were doing their best to fend off our pursuers, and we could feel the enemies' heat hard upon our backs. As we reached the base of the hill we looked up as fifteen warriors swarmed over Crum and Wheeler. One threw a musket over Crum's head and pulled it back in a chokehold, trying to drag him backwards. We watched, in absolute horror, as he was yanked to the balls of his feet. He fought back furiously and finally managed to break the man's hold when he plunged his knife into the choker's belly. We were running as fast as we could to reach him and Wheeler, but it felt as if our feet were not moving beyond a walk; it was as though we were moving sluggishly through a drowsy dream. Time slowed even further as I saw a heavy tomahawk swing and cut away nearly half of Wheeler's face. Still, he fought on, his giant body swinging his broken musket in blind hatred at those attempting to capture him. Finally, a warrior painted entirely black stepped forward, dodged one of Wheeler's swings, and smashed in his skull with a war club. Crum was not faring much better. We stopped and attempted to fire on his attackers, but they were all so near that we feared striking him. Fehn crouched at my side and sighted on the warrior nearest to Crum and brought him down with his deadly rifle. The five remaining warriors circled Crum and one gave him a sharp blow to the back of his head with war club. Crum's knees buckled, and he slumped forward into the grasp of several warriors. Quickly he was dragged over the hill and away from our view, and we continued to try to rush to him. But twenty warriors appeared above us, from behind the ridge over which Crum had disappeared, and presented their muskets in our direction. They began firing, and we jumped behind any cover that we could find; some could only press themselves to the face of the slope, clawing into it to keep from sliding backwards.

"Hobbs' Company! You bastards – to me!" we heard being shouted from somewhere behind us.

Glancing back toward the beach, we saw Major Todd taking charge of the remaining light infantry. They had been drawn up into an orderly line and were giving volley after volley into the woods. They had repelled the majority of the war party and had gained a tight defensive position. The ground between us and them was clear, but I urgently longed for us to continue up the slope in pursuit of Crum. But I could see in Lieutenant Timms' eyes what was to be done instead. I pleaded with, him but he was unshaken.

"Solomon, Pat is gone," Timms explained with great consternation. "We have to return to the troops if we're to reestablish some order. I don't want to leave him any more than you do, but there's nothing we can do for him if we get ourselves killed now. As evil as those sons of whores are, he's likely already dead …"

Timms paused and wrenched himself into a semblance of composure.

"Hobbs' Company!" he barked. "Back to the formation."

His words trailed off in a breath of defeat, and the hellish fog of dismay enshrouded me as I joined the men in a slow, reluctant trot back to the encampment.

"Solomon, damn it! Keep your musket up and watch those woods. We're not out of this thing yet!" Timms yelled at me.

I met his gaze with anger. I could not believe that we had left our brother behind. Yet I knew Timms was acting for the best of all; it was a horrible reality, disgusting to swallow. I scanned the woods, and then back where we had last seen Crum. Nothing. When we were safely behind the ranks of regular soldiers, I emptied my stomach. One of Todd's men was watching me. As I bent over, wiping off my mouth, I heard him make soft, cackling laughter at my expense. I drew myself to my full height and walked over to him as he was looking away. As I came close, I could hear him jabbering something about my lack of strength to his closest fellow. They turned as I approached, and the one who had insulted me had his mouth fixed in a stupid grin.

"Hey lad, got caught trying to hide did ya?" the soldier said through his mocking smile.

The last noises that I heard were his nose crunching as I slammed the butt of my musket into his face – and the meaty slap of his fellow's musket as he struck me in the side of the head.

It was morning when I began to wake. My vision was filled with the branches of a tree and a single robin; I could hear her singing her lilting song, though it seemed piercing and distorted. I tried to lift my head, but piercing pain ran through the edges of my face and down my back.

"Easy, Solomon," Fehn said as he pressed a wet rag to my face. "Bastard Todd wanted to hang you while you were still out; he still might. Damn, you scattered the face of that other fellow."

I looked up at him as he smiled and recounted what had happened after I was knocked on the head. He said a full-blown fight had nearly erupted between the rangers and the infantry, and Todd was most enraged that he had nearly lost control of his men while still trying to guard against the war party's return. Fehn had an egg-shaped lump on the front of his head that nearly matched the one I imagined was on the back of mine.

"Sounds like we'll all be brought up on charges, but when the boys saw you get hit, they all jumped in to help. If those warriors were still watching us, they probably thought we were all mad," Thomas said through his laughter, which made him grimace and pull the cold rag from my face and press it to his own affliction. "Timms is off with Todd right now. He's trying to work out what we're going to do from here. The war party made off with all of our prisoners, and Todd said he isn't leaving until we regain them. Then there's the matter with Crum ..."

At this, I did sit up – and felt my vision blur as the pain surged over me and the edges of my vision rushed inward. I fought off nearly passing out and stared at Fehn.

"Solomon," he continued, "we didn't find Pat or his body up there – and I looked. *Hard*, damn it. I could see where someone or something was dragged away, probably Crum. I found one of his moccasins and his knife, but nothing else. I followed their trail for about a half mile but didn't find any other sign of him except that drag mark. And it kept going further still … "

"Well – we have to go find him," I sputtered.

I started to stand but felt a warm, dark veil float down, enveloping me. I awoke a while later; my head pounded out a steady throb that matched my heartbeat. I couldn't move my head without overwhelming pain piercing into me, so when I heard someone approaching, I could only roll my eyes to see who it was. The next time I did so, Lieutenant Timms stood over me; I was looking at the shin of a dirty brown legging. I rolled my eyes back up and saw him standing there with a hint of a smile upon his face.

"Solomon, you bastard. I think I just cut a deal with the Devil to keep Todd from stretching your neck," Timms said. "I know that the right thing to do in this case is for us to return to Niagara to get fresh troops, but I agreed to not go against Major Todd's pride if he agreed to drop his charges against us. Seems he has some idea that we're going to catch up to that war party, about which, incidentally, we have no idea – of their numbers, if they have reinforcements, or if they have some strong place nearby. But, damn Todd, he knows that if he crawls back to Sir William Johnson now he'd be lucky to at best only lose his commission. So, we brave idiots will be, in short order, tromping through the woods toward God knows what – and against what the Devil may deal."

"And Crum?" I asked, in utter disbelief that Timms had not mentioned him. I knew at once that I had judged – and spoken – too soon. The look that John returned me let me know that he, too, had been thinking of Pat, and his lighthearted countenance took on a vision of somber reflection. With his thumb and his first finger, he pinched his lips and slightly rocked his head to and fro. I continued to stare up at him as he stared beyond me.

The remnants of Hobbs' Company were by then all standing near. Porter came up and kicked me lightly in the ribs and thanked me for the cracked teeth and broken nose. He was nearly as tall as Captain Hobbs had been, and as I looked up at his mangled face, I realized that he bore a close resemblance. Looking at him brought back a thousand mired memories. I closed my eyes and sifted through them all, beginning at the start of this journey and drifting through all that had occurred in this short while. It was simply unimaginable how much had transpired and what gigantic changes had taken place in a span that before would only have resulted in the planting, growth, and reaping of a few crops. I opened my eyes again; Timms was still hovering over me. He was still pinching his lip but had now also arched his back and seemed to be seeking in the clouds an answer that all were now awaiting. Finally, he spoke.

"Brothers. Major Todd plans on chasing these painted devils through their own land. The Bible tells us that *'pride cometh before the fall.'* That is what is about to occur here," Timms said. "He will gladly send us to the slaughter to satisfy his whims and needs and he will think nothing of it when he has returned to his fancy garrison in Boston with his lovely wife."

Timms stated this last while sweeping a glance over me.

"Boys," he continued, "we are to be murdered in this endeavor. I know it and see its approach in the mad look in Todd's eyes; he is without reason and shouts down any word of advice from his subordinate officers. But I have given my word that I would trade our pardon for his insane endeavor. The camp will be quiet tonight, and glaring holes will be evident in our security. It would be possible for men to slip through the lines if they were careful."

He cautiously spoke this last line, making eye contact with each of the men as he said it; all knew the meaning.

"I cannot ask you to throw your lives away on my words," he said. "For those of you who will stay, I need time to decide what the best course of action will be. So for now, get some rest."

With that, Lieutenant Timms turned and walked away. Each man looked at his fellows and tried to decide what the others were thinking.

Night soon began to fall, and the comforting sounds of the creatures in the woods let us know that no one was lurking. Before the sun set, Porter and Fehn extinguished our fire; throughout the camp, others did likewise. Whelan sat on the stump that Crum had yesterday dragged from the woods and used his knife to whittle at a scrap of boat plank he had found on the beach. The stump was next to where I lay on my blankets, still recovering from my injuries. Most of the pain had passed, its subsidence aided by some rum that Whelan had miraculously procured.

"We've buried all of the dead. I didn't even know Wheeler – did he have a family?" asked Whelan.

It struck me that we had endured that entire siege but had been so constantly involved in our duties from the time we left Fort William Henry that some of us had barely known each other – and yet we had placed our lives in each other's hands.

"Lockridge had a daughter. I know that, but I never really talked to Wheeler in the past few months," Whelan continued falteringly. "They've had us so scattered about that we didn't really meet."

"I ... I don't know, Whelan," I gasped.

I was now able to sit up, albeit with great difficulty. I rubbed the knot on the back of my head and gave a wince to the pain it produced, but it nonetheless felt much better than it had before. I got to my feet for the first time since I had been knocked from them and stared around me as the soldiers prepared for watch or bed. Standing rekindled the pounding in my head, but I was able to tolerate it and I knew that I needed to get myself prepared for the coming days.

I found Timms standing at the far eastern end of our camp. He was leaning on his musket, and he turned when he heard me walking up behind him.

"Solomon, you shouldn't be up yet," he scolded. "You took a hell of shot to the head."

I waved him off and took up a position at his side. He gazed back out over the water and then to the hill where Crum had been captured. I stepped in front of him and turned to meet his gaze.

"Crum is still alive, John," I declared flatly.

"I know," he said softly. "We failed him."

Despite his attempts to hide them, I could see by the budding starlight that tears were filling his eyes. I placed a hand on his shoulder and could feel him gently shaking.

"Not yet, Lieutenant," I assured him.

John turned and saw that I had wrapped my old gray matchcoat around my shoulders and had my haversack hanging at my side.

"If I leave, Todd will think nothing of it and will probably be happy to be rid of the final Indian amongst his ranks. I'm going for Crum," I explained.

Timms began to protest, but I continued.

"You know as well as I do that if they know we are coming they'll kill him quick so that they can move fast," I said. "They'll never know that I'm coming."

Timms knew this to be true, but inside he battled between the possibility of losing another man and the likelihood of my capability to do what I thought I could.

"I'll track them," I offered. "Try to get Todd to follow the same path, and we will meet up somewhere in between."

Lieutenant Timms began again to shake his head in dissent, but I finished our debate.

"I'm going," I said. "I have a greater chance than anybody because there is nothing but Indians between us and where we need to go. The Creator will look after me. *Maya-we-helan* – everything is as it should be."

Timms' face took on that solid resolve that I had seen so many months ago on our first meeting. He repeated my words to me and then felt under my arm for my horn. He pulled the stop out and did the same to his own. He slowly tipped his horn and topped mine off, then recapped both horns. Next, he dug into his pouch and gave me a dozen extra balls and two new flints. Finally, he instructed me to remain a minute and then walked to camp. He returned with my bow and quiver of arrows. He helped sling them over my shoulder and then drew me near.

"God's speed, Solomon," he uttered urgently. "Get Crum."

With that I turned and, seeing no sentry, slipped into the woods at the base of Crum's hill. Climbing to the top, I looked around and quickly made out the drag marks and the war party's trail. Guided by starlight and by instinct, I fell into a slow run that took me – so I swore and hoped and prayed – with every step closer to Crum's release.

XXV.

The first miles passed quickly, though not without some difficulty. The injury to my head nagged me, and several times I was made to stop and dip my head into streams to cool off the incredible heat that I felt emanating from the inside of it. As the night wore on, I lost the aid of the stars when thick clouds closed in and the threat of a storm was heralded by distant thunder. At one point, I totally lost the trail and began to feel raw panic welling up inside my deepest recesses. I sat down and closed my eyes, trying to focus. I remembered a time like this when Crum and I were scouting near Fort William Henry and I had gotten disoriented. Crum had taken my arm and pulled me close to ground. With his finger he had silently traced the horizon that is created where the trees meet the forest floor. His finger stopped on a place about twenty yards out. There, squinting, I saw where the leaves were very different than those surrounding them. They were turned and pushed up; showing where someone had passed through them. This could not be seen while looking straight at them – but upon placing my head to the ground their difference from those surrounding them was amazingly obvious. Remembering this moment, I rolled to my side and slowly opened my eyes. There, running at an angle from me, lay the trail. Something else was there, as well – almost completely covered by leaves, but clearly foreign. Crawling to it, I discovered one of Pat's leg ties that Abigail had made for him. I knew it as well as if I had made it myself. I held it a short while, running my thumb over the intricate weave. Abigail's ties were so well made that they would not fall off unless someone had purposely untied them. Looking around, I realized that my disorientation had been no careless mistake. It was a strange area, crossed by three ravines and many game trails; even an experienced tracker could become lost in this place. I knew then, for certain, that Pat was alive and aware. Still on my knees, I looked around still more closely and found small, charred twigs that were the scattered remnants of a fire. I dropped the twigs, shoved the leg tie into my pouch, and started off in a run along the trail that Pat had indicated. My footsteps in the leaves were soon joined by the patter of rain drops hitting them from above.

As I burst over the third ridge since finding Pat's leg tie, I found myself standing on a well-traveled path. There grew a huge cherry tree where the war party's trail met a main path; the tree's crisp bark had been carved away to show the blood-red wood underneath. Cut into the trunk were the designs used to indicate a war party's deeds in battle. It showed that they had killed ten men and captured three. To give greater warning to those who might find the totem was a blond scalp, stretched on a wooden hoop. The rain falling on it showed its freshness, as the water mingled through the hair and dripped out at the lock's ends in light red droplets. The emerging daylight caught the color of the droplets as they splashed down near my sodden moccasins.

The rain was becoming more persistent, so before heading off, I pulled the string from my bow and pushed it inside my shirt to save it from becoming useless. Turning, I started down the trail with greater caution, as the prospect of running into another person on this well-worn trail seemed a strong likelihood. Lightning flashed across the sky and cut through the thick canopy above me. Conditions were becoming perilous as the storm grew in its ferocity, and I was in desperate need of shelter. Pressing on, I came to a large sycamore growing near a shallow creek. Its north side was split open at the bottom to reveal a small cave. I had to crouch to enter it, but once inside saw that it provided good cover from the falling rain. The pain in my head and the exhaustion from crossing so many miles overwhelmed me as I wrapped my gray matchcoat around my soaked body; quickly I was asleep.

I am unaware as to how many minutes or hours passed until I was shaken from my sleep by the sounds of voices outside the tree. The thickness of the trunk made it impossible to decipher the language or proximity of the voices, so I remained silent and felt the knot of fear twisting in my stomach. The only thing that became certain was that the voices were not moving, and I supposed that they had stopped at the stream to refresh themselves. Craning my neck, I saw a hole in the side of the tree about ten feet above me. I hung my bow and quiver on the ramrod of my firelock and braced it against the inside of the tree so that someone looking straight into the entryway would not see them. I then pressed my back to the inside of tree and used my feet to climb to the hole. When I reached the tiny opening, I cautiously looked out over the heads of twenty Indians. To my delight, I heard the language of the Delaware, and my heart pounded hard in my chest. The apparent leader of these men was a gray-haired fellow whose sweeping locks lay down over his shoulders. In his hair he wore a tall, red roach, and over his shoulder was slung a split oak quiver. His hands were clutched together, a tall bow standing balanced beneath them. Presently, he was addressing his warriors, and all seemed enraptured with what he had to say. Clearly this man held weight with these men. To his utter surprise, the large tree to his right hailed him.

"Grandfather!" I shouted through the small hole.

The younger warriors spun up, and I was met by several firelocks and the amazed stare of the older man. With a wave of his hand, he lowered the barrels of the raised muskets and came to stand underneath the tree, looking up.

"Grandson, why are you inside the tree? Did it eat you?" he questioned in a surprised but humorous tone. "I have heard of such things."

"I was caught in the storm this morning and sought shelter here," I explained.

"Well, come down from there and we will smoke awhile," Grandfather offered in a kindly manner.

When I was down and comfortably seated by their fire, they explained that a war party, made up of Huron and Abenaki, had just passed through this area, and that word was spreading that they had captives to burn. Grandfather explained that, while he and his men had not become involved in this squabble, they were going to see to this ceremony, sent by the clan mothers to get word on an event that would surely affect them. Grandfather went on to explain all that they had heard and about their travels north from their village a day away. Of particular interest to them was if the Cayuga or Seneca would retaliate against this war party that was moving through their land without permission. He and his men did not press me, and respectfully allowed me to eat, drink, and bathe myself in the stream before I returned and sat on my matchcoat in their circle. Grandfather produced a small clay pipe and lit in with a stick from the fire. He drew from it a few times and then passed it to me. Likewise, I drew from the pipe and then let it pass to the warrior beside me. The pipe traveled our circle and then returned to its elderly keeper. I sat in silence, staring at the fire. The quiet of the woods was complete, and the corners of my vision were filled by nothing more than the peaceful flitting of every kind of bird. For a moment, it seemed as though everything was well and in order. At last, I looked up and saw the reflection of the fire in every pair of eyes, each looking on me in expectation.

"Grandfather, brothers – thank you for your kindness, your food and this good tobacco," I began.

All gave agreeable grunts and nods to me.

"I have come a long way and was part of the great battle at the Niagara fort. Many times the moon has passed across the sky since last I saw my home." My voice became rigid as my thoughts revisited the past months. Looking at Grandfather, he nodded at me to continue. "Away from Stockbridge, I met some good men and they asked me to help them. I must explain that their leader had saved my sister and me from the attack on Stockbridge."

I heard several of the warriors whispering to each other and shaking their heads, recounting what each of them knew of what had happened in Stockbridge, which was inhabited by their close relatives.

"Now that the French fort is taken, we were returning home and had many French men that the English King wished to possess," I continued. "The war party that you mentioned attacked us a few days ago and carried away all of the French men."

I stopped my story to again accept the pipe from Grandfather. At my pause, one of the warriors across the fire spoke to me.

"If all you said is so, than they were right to have attacked you and the English," he suggested. "It would be best for you to go from this place and forget those French men. It is very dangerous for you to be here."

I nodded at his words and looked down at the pipe that I held in both hands.

"There is something else, Solomon?" asked Grandfather, sensing more to my tale.

"Grandfather, the words of my brother are true, and I have forgotten those French men. But the warriors have someone most precious to me," I pleaded to them. "He is my ranger brother. And not just that; he is my sister's man, and she carries in her belly his child."

My words brought gasps from the lips of each of the men as they now realized the importance of my quest. I looked back down at the pipe and listened to the many conversations that sprang among them from my plea. Grandfather alone was silent as he weighed my words. Hushing the men, he rose and looked at each of their faces. He explained his ideas on my problem, and each man listened with close respect. He told them that they were each the directors of their own fate and could choose to go home if they wished – or carry on with him in his attempt to aid his grandson in need. As we packed up our few things and I retrieved my bow, quiver, and musket from the tree, his words echoed in my mind: *The burden of our Mohican grandson should be considered as our own to help carry.*

XXVI.

Grandfather's words had persuaded his men, and none had dissented against his intentions to assist me. We spent the next hour preparing ourselves to meet the war party. We painted our faces and bodies in a way that indicated we had no ill intent against those we would meet. I had chosen to paint myself red with long black, white, and yellow stripes that ran through the red. The shiny bear grease mixed with the dry paint powders, and in short time none of us held the same appearance that just an hour ago we had possessed. To better show our intentions, Grandfather pulled a long white wampum belt from a pouch at his waist and allowed it to hang nearly to the ground.

Still we were wary as we approached the war party's camp. In surreal fashion, as we approached the camp, we were stopped by French soldiers standing guard. Apparently those who had been freed had reestablished their former military pose and had assisted their Indian allies in presenting a good, defensive posture. A Huron warrior saw our approach and came to Grandfather to question our intent. He looked us over and then accepted the wampum belt that Grandfather held. The warrior carried it away and then returned a short while later to motion us through the French guard post. I attempted to remain discreet as my eyes searched the perimeter of the camp, trying to find Crum. When I did, my heart sank. He was lashed to a large pole that was stuck in ground and surrounded by a high pile of dry limbs. His head hung down with his chin touching his chest, and his blood had stained nearly every part of his clothing; he had not gone easily.

The Huron warrior was leading us to the center of the camp, and we were being watched by every warrior and soldier in sight. As we passed near to where Pat was being held, the warrior pointed and laughed at him. Next, the warrior motioned for us to gather around Pat. When we had formed a semicircle around him the warrior began kicking Pat's foot until he finally looked up. I fought the urge to look away from his broken and bloody face.

"Ranger! Ranger!" the warrior said in broken English. "Look at all of these men who have come to see you burn."

He then launched into more fits of menacing laughter. Pat's red-rimmed eyes stared at the warrior with abject hatred. He then scanned the lot of us standing around him, and I was thankful that he did not recognize me. His head swiveled back toward the Huron warrior in a bobbling roll that reminded me of someone profoundly drunk. When he locked his gaze on the warrior, Pat struck out his foot and kicked a plume of dirt that showered the man across his chest. The warrior reacted immediately, drawing his metal ramrod from his musket and using it to slash at Crum's face with great arcing blows. Welts rose from Pat's face, but when the beating was over he simply returned his stare in unbroken defiance. The warrior, satisfied with the beating he had handed Crum, began laughing again and then motioned us to follow him. As I passed by, I looked down at him, and he met my eyes with recognition. He gave me a slight, almost unperceivable nod – and, I swear, a small, fiendish grin.

We gathered near a large body of French and Indian men who were immersed in some sort of council. The Huron that I took to be the Indian war captain approached Grandfather, who held the white wampum belt in his hands. The two greeted each other, and we were then invited to sit among the warriors and soldiers. I looked about me to be certain that I was not near any of the soldiers who might remember me from the fort. Satisfied that I did not seem to be gathering any of their attention, I sat with my Delaware friends. Food and jugs of water were brought to us, and we were treated like old acquaintances. When we had refreshed ourselves, the war captain questioned Grandfather about our journey and why we had come here. Grandfather explained our intentions and all appeared to be satisfied with his answer. The war captain then asked if we were interested in buying some British soldiers. To Grandfather's credit, he remained incredibly unmoved by this request. He explained that we were carrying little in the way of value and that he supposed the cost would be very high. Grandfather then stated that he might like to know, out of curiosity, how much they were asking for the soldiers. The war captain smiled broadly and stated that, because these were great heroes from the Niagara battle, he could not sell them for less than fifteen pounds each. To accent their value he called to some warriors standing nearby. These warriors pulled the two British soldiers from behind a large tree and rushed them before us. Their redcoats had been stripped from them and their hands were tightly bound in front. It was clear that they had been poorly treated in the past few days. Thick blood was caked to their arms and matted their hair. These men looked as do those who have so closely visited with Death.

"As I have said, I have nothing of great value with which to buy them," Grandfather said in a dismissive tone as he returned to his food.

The war captain frowned and then sent the men to be put back to their tree.

"And how much for the ranger?" questioned Grandfather as he pointed back to Crum.

The war captain's face drew stern and he shook his head, slowly.

"He must burn in the fire to cover over the sadness of the men for the one that he killed at the soldier camp," explained the war captain.

"Ah," exclaimed Grandfather, "as it should be!"

A pipe was prepared and lit with a coal from the small fire that burned at the center of our circle. The warriors fell silent as the pipe was passed. The French officers quietly walked away upon seeing the opening of this most curious ceremony. While the pipe made its way around, my mind raced with ideas of what I might do to free Patrick. I was overcome with the sight of so many warriors. To even greater disappointment of my schemes was the tight security of the French sentries. I began to lose hope of rescuing Crum; every idea was quickly discarded out as I thought of how it would be impeded.

And then Grandfather spoke again.

"Brother," he said to the war captain. "Will you make him run the gauntlet so that we might enjoy seeing how weak this ranger is?"

It was clear that, despite all the war captain's preparations for Crum's death, this important ceremony had been not been considered. The broad smile again crossed the war captain's face as he contemplated this fitting torture.

"Grandfather, you are wise," he said with enthusiasm. "I had not thought of it, but it should be so. We will make him run between the lines so that all will see the ranger broken. When he cries out for us to stop we will take his spirit and use it to kill many more of his kind."

The war captain exclaimed with delight as he rose to his feet, clearly excited by the prospect of this great event. Grandfather returned his smile and looked to all of us who, upon receiving his gaze, were prompted to likewise smile and give out loud whoops of expectation.

When the presence of foreign men had faded from the forefront of the enemy warrior's minds, Grandfather took us aside and began to explain his plans at setting Crum free. I listened closely, but even as his wise words fell upon me and the others, we realized the near impossibility of what we were to do. Grandfather believed that if the lot of us had muskets loaded and ready we could surprise them in the darkness surrounding the nighttime gauntlet, when the warriors would be armed with little more than stout sticks and war clubs.

"Solomon, it will fall to you to be strong at the moment we bring this attack," Grandfather counseled. "Your brother is already badly off, and when he has stepped a few paces through the lines he will be in even more pain and injury."

I assured him that I would not fail them or my brother. Still, I wondered on the futility of what we were at.

The sun dipped its final plumage beneath the horizon and we secretly prepared our deceit. I double-charged my musket and made sure that my arrows would come freely from my quiver. I restored the string to my bow and felt the satisfying strength of it as I drew it back a few times. In the midst of my preparations I was moved at thoughts of the risks that my Delaware brothers were prepared to take on my behalf. I would never forget their sacrifices on this dark night.

To our advantage, just prior to the lighting of a gigantic ceremonial fire, a few warriors dragged three large barrels of rum to the center of their camp. The warriors had captured these from our camp during their raid, and they thought it a fitting time to take advantage of them and imbibe in the devilish liquid. Axes pulled from sashes were used to dash open the tops of the containers; one warrior plunged his face into an open barrel and sucked in a great quantity of the harsh rum. Warrior after warrior dipped his wooden mug into the open casks, and the Indians became furious in their drunken state. Some of them staggered from the barrels to give out hellish beatings to the prisoners, preludes to the horrible deeds that would soon be dealt out by the light of the devils' fire.

Drumbeats filled the air, and wood was added to the fire with furious delight. It had been decided that all three prisoners would be subjected to the gauntlet. Crum was being held back as the grand ending to the night of torture, as each knew that he would die in the most glorious of manners. I realized that I would have to watch the other soldiers be beaten until the time came to save Pat. I did not relish the thought of this but considered that I must do what I could for my friend and let the others meet their fates as they came to them.

Warriors were screaming to the sounds of their drums, and black night swallowed all not held within the pyre's circle. A nod from the war captain sent a dozen warriors to the business of tearing every shred of clothing from the British soldiers and one damned ranger. In their nakedness, they were jeered by the warriors who cast every insult that they could contrive upon those hapless souls. I still doubted our success, but a strong hand on my shoulder and a look from Grandfather gave me reassurance. The crack of a stick against bare flesh heralded the beginning of the gauntlet as the first soldier was sent down between our opposing lines. Those standing at the beginning of the lines were armed with sticks barely thicker than a man's finger, but as he continued through the beating, he was met by ever larger sticks – and then staffs, and then clubs. Halfway down the lines he staggered and fell, whereupon he was swarmed and struck at repeatedly until finally he was lifted and sent further down the path. He managed to fend off some of the blows by covering his head with his arms. Consequently, those limbs were cut to shreds by the striking warriors, and he only received a reprieve from the torture when he met the ends of the lines where he collapsed to the ground and was left there to bleed.

The next soldier stepped up, a man that I knew to be German. He was much larger than the fellow that had just passed and was able to quickly streak through the lines with surprisingly little injury. Still, large gashes and welts covered his body, and he was pushed to his knees as he stood, defiantly, at the end of his travails.

Finally, Patrick was led to the head of the lines where he stood with his arms still bound behind him. The screams and taunts reached a new fervor at the prospect of killing this brave man. The combined roar of howls, beating drums, and screaming demons filled my ears and mind and choked out every good nighttime sound. He was made to stand awhile as the warriors refreshed themselves with great gulps of rum, made to look down the corridor of death and weigh his lot. When the war captain was sufficiently happy that all were prepared for this venture, he strode up behind Crum and drew forth a huge sword that he had captured in his days against his English enemy. He struck down, hard, with the sword and cut the bonds that held Pat's hands. I watched as Crum brought his arms to his sides and clenched his hard fists; he was unmoved and unshaken by his nakedness or his plight. I looked to Grandfather, who quickly swept his eyes over his men to see that we all were prepared for his sign. An overly excited Huron grinned at me and shoved a huge tin mug in my direction. The tin sloshed over with rum, and he implored me to sup. I took his tin and feigned a deep drink, then quickly handed it back to him, hating this distraction from what I knew I was to be at. The war captain drew back the sword and I tensed, thinking that he might behead Pat before he had an attempt to run. Instead, the captain struck him with the flat of the blade, and Crum took off like a shot, knocking men down as he plowed through his would be-executioners. Still, the blows met his skin – but as he neared us we discreetly stepped back from the lines. Grandfather and the other Delawares each grabbed the man closest to them and gently drew them near in mock motions of friendship. With a warrior in each of their embraces, they quietly slit these mens' throats and then held them from falling. When Pat was but a pace away I stepped strongly forward and jammed the end of my musket, discharging it as I did so, into the man who had just offered me his cup. This sent him reeling to the ground with a look of unexpected surprise blazing over his jovial countenance. My fellows dropped the warm corpses like drunken lovers and likewise fired into the flanks of the war party, ending their joy and mirth. I wrapped my arm around the back of Pat's neck and drew him toward me. He, not knowing me, struck out with a fist into my stomach, blowing the air from my chest.

"Pat, it's me," I pleaded quickly.

His face came up to mine and he realized what was happening.

"Solomon!" he cried. "Let's get the hell out of here."

The warriors were quickly becoming aware of what had happened, and suddenly they turned their fury on my brothers. We dragged ourselves into a tight knot with Pat at our center. Pat lashed out and pulled the German to us as we fought our way to the edge of the camp. The suddenness of our rebellion had given us but a brief advantage, and we were immediately surrounded, my worst predictions coming true. It would only take a few moments for us to be overwhelmed, and my mind raced as we fought with all our might against the war party. It was then that I heard the sweetest sound that could have erupted in all the woods of North America.

"WAKE UP THE DEAD, ME BOYS!" Screamed Lieutenant Timms from the edge of our darkness.

This brought a hail of lead into our attackers, mowing them like hay and further disorienting them. My Delaware brothers drew down their heads as we rushed to the ranks of Hobbs' Company. Some of their number fell in our rush, and they were snatched away by what seemed a large, unseen hand. The war party was preparing to turn on Hobbs' when another volley, this dealt out by the rest of

Todd's hat men, struck them from the far edge of their camp. With so many killed or injured in the initial shots, the number of Huron, Abenaki, or French men able to fight seemed greatly diminished.

"By company, fix bayonets!" came the shout over the din of the enemies' wails – screams now given out in pain having replaced the prior whoops of victory and vengeance.

"*CHARGE!*" continued the English orders.

The charge of the light infantry was nearly palpable to us, as even those who were allies to this vicious, unified monster – brandishing dozens of sharp spines and impaling all who lay in its path – tried to move far away from its onslaught. Hobbs' Company did not hold such a tight formation, but still we retained some semblance of order as, beginning back-to-back, we created an ever-expanding ring, giving out Indian play to the original owners of this fashion of fighting. I handed Pat my musket, pouch, and horn, and he stood, without a stitch of cloth but wearing great open wounds and welts, working the King's Arm. The war captain was attempting to rally his men; I saw massing, across the clearing, a huge horde of men who had recovered their senses and their muskets.

"Lieutenant, there!" I shouted to Timms as I sent an arrow in their direction.

He craned his neck to see the gathering that I had spied, and Fehn shifted over in front of him to discharge a fiery belch of lead into several rushing warriors. The loud report made me look past Timms, and I saw the great smoking mouth of Thomas' blunderbuss as he dumped more powder and a handful of shot, rocks, and the shards of a broken mirror down its throat. Fehn reshouldered the short gun and fired another time, cutting a swath through the crowd pressing in on us. Another quick glance showed me Whelan taking big steps and swings with a long-handled, spiked axe. The slender point would barely enter the body of a man before Whelan retracted it and cleaved with the heavy blade at the other side of the shaft. A pile of dead and dying men formed around our circle.

I heard a great war cry and turned in time to see a warrior painted half red and half black running up the backs of several of his injured fellows. He gained the air above us in an unbelievable leap. He came down with incredible force near the center of our circle, and the sharp edge of his tomahawk bit deep into my arm, causing a loud cracking noise to enter my ears and turn my stomach. Blood instantly gushed from the tear in my flesh, causing me to instinctually drop my bow and clench a hand over my wound. Now the warrior clenched his tomahawk in both hands and rose up on the balls of his feet, then struck down with all the strength he could muster. Instinctually, I flinched away – but was happy to hear the sound of his blade dully striking wood rather than my spine. As I staggered backwards, I saw Crum throw aside my musket, which had been deeply pierced by warrior's tomahawk. Pat jumped on the man like Satan's own naked imp and shoved him to the ground in a great doubled mass. His hands worked quickly as he snatched the stunned warrior's knife from a sheath about the painted neck and slashed open his ribs and stomach, spilling out all of the gore. Pat rose from the doomed man and kicked at the tomahawk stuck in my musket until the handle broke away from the head. Pat then proceeded to grasp the firelock by the muzzle end and beat the eviscerated warrior, causing great splashes of blood to spray over himself and me. As Sergeant Crum dashed out this man's brains, he emitted a chest-rattling growl, indiscernible from that of a bear. Rising from his quarry, he gave out another, even louder growl as high over his head he held the crimson musket in one hand and the dead man's knife in the other. This second growl startled those who had not just witnessed his victory, and this half-second is one of those forever burned into my memory: that of all Hobbs' Company glancing over their shoulders and the looks on their faces at the wailing, blood-covered devil in their midst.

The moment passed faster than it had come when a mass of balls flew through our company, cutting several of our men and Delaware brothers down. The re-formed Indian party, led by the war captain, had begun their attack on us. The drunken heathens that we had previously been beating away were replaced by those with clearer heads and loaded guns.

Things grew worse as we fended off the fresh attack. We spied the light infantry, who had lost the momentum, and hence the advantage, gained in their surprise attack. Redcoats were falling in startling numbers and we were so far separated as to not be able to go to their aid – nor they to ours. When the events seemed most dire – indeed, completely without hope – the tide of our destiny was again turned, this time by the arrival of a large party of Iroquois. To our great relief, they had overheard the ensuing battle and had come to investigate, finding their troubled English brothers in need. What unfolded occurred with such swiftness that I was unable to follow the complete gradation of events. There was more shooting, more screams, more blood – and then, there was stillness. And within short order the combined body of Seneca, Mohawk, and Oneida had gathered together most of the surviving Huron and Abenakis and immediately sentenced them to death for their intrusion on Iroquois land. As Lieutenant Timms wrapped the wound to my arm, a dreadful sight filled my eyes. Dozens of Huron and Abenaki were dragged to the execution fire – that which had earlier been constructed for the sake of the British soldiers – and tied to nearby to posts. The Iroquois warriors heaped branches, sticks, logs, and even the Huron's and Abenaki's personal belongings upon the captured men. So terrible and all-consuming was their anger at these intruders that no mercy was to be found as the feverish massacre was laid in place. My protests were violently stopped by Timms and

Crum, as they explained that, without the intervention of the Iroquois, the Huron and Abenaki would presently be feasting on my brothers' hearts.

We had been saved, but at what horrible cost? Despite all that I had witnessed and done, I clung with unyielding fingers to my gentle soul. I desired, more than anything at that moment, to be in Catherine's embrace, where I would bury my head and cast out all evil thoughts and images; the grotesque feeding of dark ways was overwhelming, and I realized that I was not in a place befitting those who sought a good path. I held to this thought as the screams of tortured men fought to overcome my sanity, and I came to the realization that, as unfortunate and unfair as it may seem, sometimes those bearing light souls are forced into the darkness. I hoped that it was with purpose, maybe so that we could see how brightly our lights really shined. My head spun amid the rapid turn of events, the toss from saved to sacrificed to saved again was more switching than any spirit should be able to withstand. My thoughts for the sacrificed were flooded away by an explosion of pain as John and Pat gave a final, hard tug at the bandage they had placed around my arm. I was told that the degree of tightness was due to the amount of blood that might otherwise lose to the deep wound. I was thankful for their attendance to the wound, but my attempts to voice my gratitude were cut short as the stress, exhaustion, and my many injuries collided and drew me into the darkness.

While my mind was gone from the hell around me, I dreamt of Stockbridge in its restored state. My unscarred body drifted through the tall reeds that bordered the Housatonic River, and I could smell the sweet water that rippled over the rocks in trickling whispers. My eyes passed over deadly snakes that lay in ambush along the shore, but they had no effect, they could not reach me. I dismissed them and came to a lovely place along the banks of the river where my head filled with tunes that I had carried in my heart for many years.

These songs and the image of her face had been relief when none other was to be had, food when I was famished, and release from my thirst when I was parched. Just as I glimpsed the face of my love, I was torn from sleep and made to face the waking world's atrocities once again.

The night was long, and to this day I have trouble recalling what occurrences were real and which were concocted by my imagination. The rank, disgusting smells and the smoke of the terrible eve lingered everywhere as we ambled about the camp in directionless awe. Lieutenant Timms and Sergeant Crum conferred with the leaders of the Iroquois so that they could devise the best way to continue east. Major Todd was present at this conference, as well, but he held the look of a man who had utterly lost all sense. Few of his men remained – only enough to man a few of the boats and bear away the three French captives who had been spared the slaughter. The Iroquois agreed to escort us to our landing; then they would need to return to their villages or hunt down the Huron and Abenaki who had escaped the night's vengeance. Our procession ambled slowly, as no man was without a few injuries. Indeed, the fighting had been so concentrated that none were seen who were not shot, cut, stabbed, or burned. The Iroquois gathered up any unburned plunder, as no soldier or ranger desired a thing to slow him from his homes. In his crazed state of mind, Major Todd began marching his troops in rank and file as if they were on parade. All cast questioning looks to one another at this, but did not see the harm of it – and neither did they desire to create any further strife, as we were so close to returning.

When the Iroquois had left us to attend to our boats, Major Todd called Timms to him. He asked him if the "savage" that moved in his ranks was the same who had earlier deserted. Lieutenant Timms explained that I had gone off in hopes of tracking the war party and that I had been successful in my endeavor. Just the same, Todd said, I would now accompany his light infantry so that he could keep a watchful eye on me. He also informed Timms that I must be brought up for charges. As mystified as John was by what Todd was telling him, Timms decided that it would be best that we do as he said so that strife could be held to a minimum until we could gain some fort and he could explain to a higher officer all that had happened. He told me to go with the light infantry, but that he would be ever-watchful for any injury that Major Todd might try to deal me.

And so it was that my fate once again came to be clutched in the claws of my mortal foe.

XXVII.

"Watch that bastard," Crum warned before we struck off from the shore.

I told him that I would, and he said that he'd make sure that none came close to me. I thanked him and then climbed into the boat that bore Major Todd, the prisoners, and several of the light infantry. Before long, a strong wind aided our sail east. I reserved those first moments of smooth advance to say a few hopeful prayers for my brothers' safe return, for fine, happy receptions, and for my own soul's preservation.

At the end of our first day on the lake, Major Todd ordered us ashore near the mouth of a large bay. After we came to shore, Todd, in his fear of another ambush, ordered us rangers to immediately prepare for a scout of the entire area near our landing. I was relieved to be restored to my former place as scout for Hobbs' Company. We ranged ahead of the regular soldiers, branching out and making our way through the woods in a most easy manner, as each man knew all the others' ways and thoughts. Major Todd's madness found a new fervor as he ordered us further and further inland. Lieutenant Timms grew irritated at this unnecessary mistreatment of the severely battered soldiers and rangers. My own injury had made it nearly impossible for me to carry my musket without experiencing great ripples of pain, but I weathered our movements without complaint, knowing we were so close to being away from this thing. After pushing almost three miles inland we came to a large trail, and I was sent to investigate. I was surprised when, shortly, I came across a large Indian village that was well situated. The village sustained many inhabitants and numerous large fields of plentiful corn. By watching from a distance, I was able to identify the people living there as Delaware and I was greatly relieved to know that a large body of my relatives was so near at hand. I returned to Lieutenant Timms with my findings, and Major Todd broke away from his infantry to listen in on my news. His eyes darted about wildly, and Timms and I feared what he might say. Our fears were not without warrant, as in his next breath he ordered that we should move upon this village in a strong fashion to see to their doings. I explained again that they were friends and that there was little need for us to raise their alarm, but Major Todd insisted in his command. Subsequently we were placed in a stance of great aggression and sent into the village, bringing great consternation to those peaceable people. Todd sent men to search out the various wigwams and huts of the villagers, and I felt greatly humiliated at this trespass against these innocent folks.

For Todd's own part, he went off alone – and none had seen him in quite a while when Timms called for me to seek him out. I had searched a dozen places when I came up to a wigwam that lay near the very edge of the village. As I neared it, I could hear soft whimpers coming from inside, and I grew cautious at these sounds. My thumb eased the cock of my firelock back, and I walked very near to the back of the wigwam to try to listen to what was occurring within. Slowly, I walked around the hut and could hear the crying in ever louder succession as I drew near the entrance. Furtively, I pulled aside the deerskin that draped over the doorway and crept in. My eyes took time to adjust to the smoky darkness, and when they had, I was presented with the pale skin of Major Todd's bare back. My eyes shifted about as I took in his coat that had been tossed aside and his sword that was lying on top of it. Again, I heard the soft cries – they were coming from in front of

Todd. He wheeled about to see to the intrusion on his actions. When he turned sideways, I saw a young girl, no more than fifteen summers old, huddled before him. Her dress had been torn from her and her bare breasts were red from abuse.

"Scout, I've no need for your assistance here. Return to your company and I'll be along shortly. I'm merely enjoying the fruits of the forest," Todd said as a maniacal grin parted his lips.

All that I felt – and hated – about this man welled up violently inside me in those moments, and I met the gaze of the injured girl. Her stare held such horror that I nearly wept at knowing what was happening. The pains that I bore in my body in no way compared to the hideous circumstances that I was discovering in that moment of sickening revelation.

"Scout, you have created more than enough trouble for yourself, but I might find mercy in my heart for your discretions if you leave this instant," Todd shouted at me.

With that, he turned back to his prey. Red fury filled my mind, making my head to reel. The clatter of my musket to the hard earthen floor made Todd turn about yet again as he watched me draw my tomahawk from behind my back.

"*BOY, WHAT ARE YOU ABOUT?*" he screamed as he met my murderous eyes.

"To hell with you!" I screamed back as I rushed forward, giving a great war cry and burying the head of my tomahawk deep into his chest.

The force of my blow swung him about-face, and he clambered erratically for his sword. He never reached it. I released my tomahawk and drew my knife, which I used to open deep cuts in his throat, silencing his demon tongue and evil ways forever. His mouth gaped open with unspoken words, and I heard a flurry of commotion behind me as I made my final stroke. Lieutenant Timms stood in the doorway with his musket leveled at my chest; my teeth were crushed together as I drew ragged breaths and turned to meet him. Quickly, John reviewed the scene: Todd laying bloody and dead, the naked girl cowering in the corner, and me in a furious state.

"Do what you must, brother," I said through my clenched teeth.

At first, I believed that John might shoot me. But then his features grew soft as he took in all that had happened.

"What I saw was this girl being attacked and her brother coming to her aid," Timms gave to me. "Her brother was instantly punished for his affront against the Crown."

I nodded to him and relaxed as he returned my nod. I drew a blanket from a nearby pile and wrapped it around the girl. Her cries grew sharper still as her shock subsided, and I explained to her in her language that all would be fine. She clung to me and I felt her body shake as great sobs shook her entire being. I met her gaze once again, and she thanked me a thousand times in a single breath. I felt her tight fist push against my hand and I let her place in my palm something metallic and sharp. I gripped it hard and joined John as we walked from the wigwam and began our return to the gathered British soldiers. As I walked I opened my hand and saw a beautiful French double-cross made of silver. I kept this gift and, even as I sit here placing these words to paper, wear this emblem of triumph over hate.

"We will never speak of this thing to another soul, Solomon," Timms stated with blunt finality. It became one of many secrets that he and I shared in our many years. I believe that it is the event that, above all others, bound us together as true brothers.

When we had regained the ranks of light infantry and rangers, he explained what had become of Major Todd. The few dubious looks were quickly dashed away by the adamant words of Lieutenant Timms. Some of Todd's men insisted that we give him a proper Christian burial. And so it was done, in a hasty manner beneath a tree in the surrounding woods. And as soon as possible we were then back on our way to the boats. But before we left the village, I gave to the people my most heartfelt apology at our brutal incursion; this they reluctantly accepted. I explained to them that never again would such a thing happen to them as long as I was party to the event. Their leaders gave me solemn nods, and we departed in a peaceful way.

The remainder of our journey was undertaken in a quiet and quick manner. Some of Todd's men, not knowing the true elements of what had occurred, were greatly upset at the loss of their leader. All were shrouded in memories of their departed brothers and we now moved faster than ever on our return to our homes.

The fort at Oswego heralded our approach with great blasts from its cannons. We were met by the soldiers and officers who had been based there to hold that place and await our return. They had already received news regarding our victory at Niagara but were new to what had occurred since. No one questioned the details of Major Todd's demise, and I suspected that several of the officers were relieved to be rid of him. Little time was spent at the fort, as we wished to return to our own garrison to see to our families and hearths. Our riverine and overland passage was met by no further incursions, and we came to Fort William Henry with glad hearts and mending bodies.

XXVIII.

News of our return swept quickly through the fort. We trudged up the hill and were gladly met by a large gathering of our families and friends. Namoosh bounded from the gates and nearly felled me to the ground, covering me with great nips and licks of approval. I regained my composure in time to see Abigail embrace Patrick. She held the hand of little Hannick, who stood at her side, and clutched a small babe to her breast. In the time that we had been gone she had given birth to a little boy who was bright-eyed and full of wonder at his first look at his father. No adult eyes were without tears; there were those who wept upon the safe return of their loved ones, and those who would never see their men again. I held my new nephew and in his face saw a hundred prayers answered. In my entire life I had never been more grateful to see a familiar place.

After we had settled a bit, we held a ceremony for those who had not made the return. Then we were carried away to a great feast for the survivors. From a distance, I watched as Lieutenant Timms delivered the message of Major Todd's death to Catherine. Crying, she slowly walked away after John had finished, and I began to wonder how I would speak to her – and if I would tell her the truth. Somehow, I felt disgusted that I had brought her such grief. Yet I wondered whether, if I revealed to her the double-edged truth, it would help in her anguish. My love for her had never wavered, and more than ever I wanted to comfort her; but I grappled with the question of wherein lay truer solace: confession or silence?

Days passed as we enjoyed the newfound comforts of the fort and the knowledge that the campaign to the north had been as successful as our march against Fort Niagara. The greatest thought that overwhelmed my every activity was that I needed to approach Catherine; no longer had I any other issue to occupy my mind.

I received pay for my service to the army on the second week we were at Fort William Henry. With little urgent need to procure anything else, I decided to go to the armorer and attempt to purchase the trade gun that I had originally acquired in Stockbridge. It looked far better than when I had first seen it, as it had been cleaned and oiled in the ensuing weeks. My King's Arm was given to the armorer for repair; its stock had been nearly split in two from the tomahawk cut it had received. Just before I handed it over, my finger traced along its many bumps and scars, lingering even over the huge, rough gouge where it had been broken by the enemy's blow. Then my hand lightly touched the wound to my other arm. Abigail had reset the dressing, scolding Patrick for the barbaric job that he and John had originally done.

"I brought him back to you," Patrick had said crossly. "What more do you want from me, woman?" Then he had laughed – indeed, we all did. We laughed until tears streamed down our faces. We were as close to home as any had been in too long a time.

When I picked up the trade gun, I told the armorer that I would return for the other musket when it had been repaired. The sun hung low in the sky as I exited the armory. I held up my hand to shield my eyes and looked out across Lake George. The last of the day's light threaded about the small waves' ripples and cast the arrows of tree shadows against the great pond.

"You have returned, Solomon?"

Catherine's words came to me from the first patch of night, cast by the barracks' shaded side. I turned. The view of her as a grown woman contrasted against most of the images that I held in my mind

– those, of course, being of us as children in Stockbridge. I had seen her at the fort before, of course, but then it was still through the lenses of a thousand other notions. Now, though, I truly saw her, in a manner that was at once simple and profound, immediate and infinite. We were no longer children; yet still I did not feel entirely like a man. I turned my gaze from her and back to the lake, watching as the last few drops of dappled orange disappeared from its surface.

"Almost," I said quietly.

I heard her approach and could feel the heat of my own body perceptively rise as she neared. My sleeve was rolled up past my elbow as to give my wound fresh air, and her soft fingers reached out to touch the bared and scarred skin. The tips of her fingers lingered briefly at the tear in my skin, and it was the most healing sensation that I have ever experienced from another's body. The wave of her touch seemed to run through my wound, up my veins, and across my heart. I looked back at her as large tears formed at the edges of her eyes. She was usually so strong, and it pulled at my breath to see her unhappy. I wrapped my injured arm around her and pulled her to me. Her arms likewise encircled me, and I relished the reunion with my old friend and my one true love. I closed my eyes as the smell of her filled my nose and absorbed my mind.

I recounted all of the trails that I had traversed in the preceding months and years. My mind and then my mouth retraced each wonderful and horrible thing. The images of them passed through my thoughts: the deer hunt before Stockbridge was attacked, Hobbs with his pipe, war parties slipping between trees, my hands covered in red paint before battle, the smoke of a hundred fires in camp, Catherine riding into the fort, the immense walls at Niagara, Timms, Crum, Whelan, Fehn, the company's brotherly laughter and lamentations causing others to cast upon us curious, uncomfortable glances. All of it sloshed about in my head … and now I was home with Catherine in my arms. Home, as I had heard, was the place where those you love dwelled – and that was definitely this place.

"I have returned," I said softly to Catherine as I stroked her hair in my hands and as her tears fell upon my shirt. "At last, I have returned."

XXIX.

For much time to come, I found myself ever in the company of these great people. Both bitterly and sweetly, the battles between France and England continued to rage, which afforded Hobbs' men the opportunity to keep together in our service to the Crown. And she came. Catherine threw away the life of an officer's lady and took on the lowly existence of our poor lot.

Perhaps I might write yet of these further deeds, and also of all that has transpired in my life beyond them, all that has brought me, forsaken and forgotten, to this far-off place. But the night is deep, and it draws tightly about my little cabin and close upon my soul. Outside all is silence and sleep beneath the winking starlight of my autumn sky. Perhaps I may yet recount more, but for now – and only our Father knows, perhaps forever – the embers of my hearth grow dim and cold. *We may or might never all meet here again.* And I feel that if nothing else is to be recorded of my memories, it should be these final, essential observations.

As time progressed, we members of Hobbs' company found ourselves in other conflicts – both small and large, armed and otherwise – facing ever-changing enemies and obstacles, but never trading those who stood at our sides. We may have been a "poor lot," as I have lately stated. But we were also the richest of all the men and women in the forest, as we bore possessions of true and enduring value: the warm embrace of a lover, the sturdy hand of a trusted friend on one's shoulder, the watchful eye of a brother, the mindful care of a sister, and the enchanting gleam seen within the eyes of our children. It was there that we built our ramparts and sought refuge whenever life grew hard. There that we were buffered against the storm. And it was from there, from that most fortified of positions, that we gave out our own storms against those who opposed us. Never has there roamed the forest a greater party of men and women than that comprised of my brothers and sisters, and as I pen these last few words I ask of the Creator only one favor: that someday we might all again join together in a small cabin in a corner of Heaven.

While the chroniclers of history may attempt to impart that many of the events in which we were involved held great sway in the creation or destruction of this or that nation, what truly was most important was that we found each other and discovered ourselves, and that unwaveringly we guarded our own and those we loved with sacred honor.

An accomplished historian, filmmaker, re-enactor, naturalist, and wilderness-skills instructor, William T. Johnson has traveled throughout the United States giving presentations on North American history and Eastern Woodland Indian culture. He has participated in dozens of historical reenactments and has appeared in numerous documentaries exploring crucial periods in American history. *With Sacred Honor* is Johnson's first novel. He makes his home in Ohio.

WITHDRAWN

WITHDRAWN